OROONOKO

OROONOKO:

OR, THE

Royal Slave.

A TRUE

HISTORY.

By Mrs. *A. BEHN*.

LONDON,

Printed for *Will. Canning*, at his Shop in
the *Temple-Cloysters*. 1688.

OROONOKO
or
the Royal Slave

With an Introduction by
LORE METZGER

APHRA BEHN

W · W · NORTON & COMPANY

New York · London

First published as a Norton paperback 1973; reissued 1997

Library of Congress Cataloging in Publication Data
Behn, Aphra (Amis) 1640–1689.
  Oroonoko; or, The royal slave.
  (The Norton library)
  Reprint of the 1688 ed. printed for W. Canning,
London.
  I. Title.
PZ3.B396920s3   [PR3317]   823'.4   73-17252

ISBN 0-393-31205-4

W. W. Norton & Company, Inc., 500 Fifth Avenue, New York, N. Y. 10110
W. W. Norton & Company Ltd., 10 Coptic Street, London WC1A 1PU

    4 5 6 7 8 9 0

CONTENTS

INTRODUCTION

WHEN Virginia Woolf wrote a magazine article in 1929 on "Women and Fiction," she explained the deliberate ambiguity of her title: "it may allude to women and the fiction that they write, or to women and the fiction that is written about them." [1] Her article does not mention Aphra Behn although she was both the first woman in England to make a career of writing for the theater and one of the earliest English novelists. The fiction she produced has been supplemented for two and a half centuries by a considerable amount of fiction about her. The facts of her life are so few yet so colorful that they quickly evoked sensational embellishment, insinuation, and speculation about her voyage to the West Indies, her love affairs, and her activities as a spy. The few facts suffice to establish Aphra Behn's opportunities for experience of the world of politics and art as larger and more varied than those open to any woman writer of the eighteenth or nineteenth century.

Aphra Behn had probably traveled to Surinam in the West Indies, married and probably been widowed, worked as a spy for the British crown in Antwerp, and been briefly imprisoned for debt before she turned to a literary career in 1670, first as a dramatist and then toward the end of her life as a writer of fiction. Her best known piece of fiction, *Oroonoko* (1688), also

1. *Granite and Rainbow* (London: The Hogarth Press, 1958), p. 76.

proved a popular success on the stage for a century after Thomas Southerne first presented his dramatic adaptation in 1694. And inevitably it produced its share of fictions. During her own time there were rumors that Aphra Behn had had a love affair with the black hero of her story. Our century has contributed the less sensational fictions that Mrs. Behn advanced the cause of abolitionism and that she created the first literary portrayal of the noble savage. Exaggerated though these claims are, they lead us to central questions in Mrs. Behn's "history of the royal slave," which give her work what coherence it has. Is human nobility the result of natural endowment or of education? Is it attainable only in and through European civilization? Can a high ideal of human conduct prevail in a society governed by Machiavellian principles? Though it is not a philosophical novel, Mrs. Behn's narrative clearly moves toward insights that are as close to Rousseau as to Montaigne.

The moral themes are embedded in a narrative that mixes the marvelous and the familiar, improbable incidents and realistic descriptions, into a purported "life" of Oroonoko. Aphra Behn consistently maintains the pose of reporting events to which she has either been an eye-witness or of which she has had firsthand accounts—she admits no hearsay evidence—even when she presents a character of matchless grandeur engaged in mythical encounters. She thus imposes the novelist's point of view on romance material at a time when a clear distinction between the two narrative forms was barely beginning to emerge. "Romances are generally composed of the constant loves and invincible courages of heroes, heroines, kings and queens, mortals of the first rank," wrote Congreve in 1692 in his "Preface to the Reader" to *Incognita*, "where lofty language, miraculous contingencies and impossible performances elevate and surprise the reader into a giddy delight. . . ." Novels, on the other hand, deal with the familiar, represent "intrigues in practice" and delight us with "accidents and odd events, but not such as are wholly unusual or unprecedented, such which not being so distant from

INTRODUCTION

our belief bring also the pleasure near us. Romances give more of wonder, novels more delight." [2]

Though Aphra Behn's fusion of romance motifs with novelistic verisimilitude does not consistently produce both wonder and delight, it arouses interest because its improvisational flexibility favors the exploration of favorite Renaissance themes. The opening description of the exotic birds and beasts of Surinam quickly shifts to the first of these themes, the antithesis of innocent natural and corrupt civilized man, a Renaissance commonplace in both imaginary and proportedly factual travel accounts. Aphra Behn derives from personal observation of the native Indians "an absolute idea of the first state of innocence, before man knew how to sin." Her argument that nature "better instructs the world, than all the inventions of man" rests on the traditional satiric view of the superiority of the state of nature by virtue of its ignorance of the civilized arts and artifices. The Caribs are superior to Europeans not so much on the basis of what they know as of what they do not know: "they understand no vice, or cunning, but when they are taught by the white men." They are so ignorant of lies and frauds that they inquire of the British governor "what name they had for a man who promised a thing he did not do?" [3] Thus for Aphra Behn,

2. *Incognita and The Way of the World*, ed. A. Norman Jeffares (Columbia, S. C.: University of South Carolina Press, 1965), pp. 32–33. I have modernized the spelling in this and all subsequent quotations from seventeenth century texts.

3. Montaigne's essay "Of Cannibals" was the *locus classicus* of this satiric tradition. Florio's translation of 1603 was widely read in England throughout the seventeenth century. "This is a nation," writes Montaigne of his uncorrupted commonwealth, "in which there is no sort of traffic, no knowledge of letters, no science of numbers, no name for a magistrate, or for political superiority. . . . The very words that signify lying, treachery, dissimulation, avarice, envy, belittling, pardon—unheard of." *The Complete Essays of Montaigne*, tr. Doñald M. Frame (Stanford, Calif.: Stanford University Press, 1965), p. 153.

xi

as for many another voyager, the New World offered a salutary retreat from corrupt civilization. Like Columbus, she was certain that the earthly paradise was bound to be discovered near the Orinoko River.[4]

In the central narrative, the story of the black hero, Oroonoko, Mrs. Behn departs from the clear-cut antithesis between nature and civilization. Although she still equates some of the white ruling colonists with the perverted morality of European civilization, she does not invest the black slaves with natural nobility. While she idealizes the Indians, she sees the slaves as mere objects to be bought and sold, the lucrative commodities of the slave trade. She completely accepts the institution, depicts her heroic black prince as an important trader himself, who, in his days as a great warrior, supplied captives to the English and Spanish, learning from them the languages of civilized Europe. The black slaves in this heroic romance are slavish—they prostrate themselves before Oroonoko when he appears in Surinam, worship him only to desert him, and join his persecutors when the rebellion he leads collapses.

Thus Aphra Behn distinguishes between the noble Indian savages, the brutish black slaves, and the civilized white barbarians, before elevating Oroonoko above all three groups. He emerges as the norm of human nobility because he possesses the necessary *positive* virtues and not merely the *negative* ignorance of deceit and fraud, which he shares with the innocent Indians. His surpassing courage and honor, strength and beauty of body and mind, generosity and loyalty, characterize him both in the first half of his life as a prince in Coramantien and in the second half as a slave in Surinam. The first part of the novel tells an exotic tale of the prince as a young warrior-hero, experiencing the joys and agonies of love in a series of adventures and intrigues, among them an attempted rescue of his

4. See *The Select Letters of Christopher Columbus* (London: Hakluyt Society, 1870), pp. 141–143. Defoe followed this tradition when he located Robinson Crusoe's island near the mouth of the Orinoko.

INTRODUCTION

beautiful beloved from the King's seraglio. (Like many of her contemporaries, Mrs. Behn does not distinguish between Negro and Moor, freely mixing African and Oriental habits.) While thematically this part of the narrative is less remarkable than the second, it serves to establish Oroonoko as a black prince with all the accomplishments of Castiglione's perfect courtier. There is nothing primitive or barbaric about her hero, as Mrs. Behn assures us: he has "all the civility of a well-bred great man." High-born, endowed with physical perfection and mental quickness, trained and proven in the art of warfare, tutored by a Frenchman in "morals, language and science," Oroonoko is a paradigm of the virtues and accomplishments that nature and nuture produce in a perfect collaboration. Mrs. Behn admits of no doubt that her black hero was "as capable even of reigning well, and of governing as wisely, had as great a soul, as politic maxims, and was as sensible of power, as any Prince civilized in the most refined schools of humanity and learning, or the most illustrious courts." Although this statement suggests satiric possibilities, Mrs. Behn does not measure actual rulers against this ideal in her predominantly heroic romance. But in the second half of the narrative, which depicts Oroonoko's life as a slave, she exhibits more fully the actual immoral and brutal behavior of the "civilized" colonial rulers, whom the slave Oroonoko ultimately denounces as "below the wildest savages."

Not, however, that the story of Oroonoko's life as a slave is primarily didactic or satiric. In writing fiction, as in writing plays, Aphra Behn's primary purpose was to entertain. She dissociated herself from those who defended the theater against Puritan attacks by claiming a high moral purpose for art. "In my judgement," she wrote in the prefatory epistle to *The Dutch Lover*, "the increasing number of our latter plays have not done much more towards the amending of men's morals, or their wit, than has the frequent preaching, which this last age has been pestered with. . . ." She considered a play "the best divertissement that wise men have."

INTRODUCTION

And she provided as amply for "divertissement" in *Oroonoko* as in her romantic comedy. Even Oroonoko's slavery is not without marvelous adventures and heroic exploits, particularized and localized through the detailed geography and social customs of Surinam and the presence of historical persons. The improbability of some of the adventures—such as Oroonoko's slaying of an invincible tiger that seven bullets fired into the heart had failed to kill—does not undercut the author's challenge to the smug belief in the superiority of European civilization or weaken the final passionate invective against "civilized" brutality.

In his encounters with his exploiters and oppressors Oroonoko's heroism undergoes its greatest trial, not in a contest of strength but in moral combat. Separated from his kingdom and reduced to the impotence of a plantation slave, he pits his personal code of honesty, honor, loyalty, and fortitude against the social order that sanctions self-interest, arrogant power, and sadistic brutality. He comes close to embodying Rousseau's ideal of what an early stage of human community may produce as against a decadent society governed by competitive self-interest.[5] Oroonoko believes in virtuous action voluntarily practiced among individuals. The colonial rulers believe in law-enforced supremacy that leaves morality aside. In his climactic speech on the "miseries and ignominies of slavery," Oroonoko ends by lashing out at these brutalizing wielders of legal oppression who serve ends far removed from his heroic code: "have they vanquished us nobly in fight? Have they won us in honourable battle? . . . No, but we are bought and sold like apes or monkeys, to be the sport of women, fools and cowards; and the support of rogues and runagates, that have abandoned their own countries for rapine, murders, theft and villainies. . . . And shall

5. For an illuminating discussion of Rousseau's position see Arthur O. Lovejoy's article, "The Supposed Primitivism of Rousseau's *Discourse on Inequality*," *Essays in the History of Ideas* (New York: Capricorn Books, G. P. Putnam's Sons, 1960), pp. 14–37.

INTRODUCTION

we render obedience to such a degenerate race, who have no one human virtue left, to distinguish them from the vilest creatures? Will you, I say, suffer the lash from such hands?" By depicting the aborted slave rebellion, Oroonoko's inhuman tortures, and his death by dismemberment, the final pages of the novel suggest that his heroic ideals cannot prevail in the real world. While not turning the narrative into an anti-romance, Aphra Behn's realistic assessment of the possibilities of the ruthless exercise of power prevents her offering a conclusion in which her hero either successfuly leads the slave insurrection or effectively avenges himself on his tormentors. Although it suggests a realistic view counter to heroic idealism, *Oroonoko* remains to the end a heterogeneous blend of realism and romance, a tale of fabulous adventures anchored in vivid social particularities, told by a charmingly intrusive narrator. Our interest in this omnipresent eye-witness is heightened by our awareness that Aphra Behn was the first woman to compete successfully with men in the theatrical world, claiming for both her private life and public work the same right to social and artistic proprieties and improprieties that Restoration London accorded to male dramatists. In her greatest stage success, *The Rover*, she asserted her iconoclastic views of the woman's place in society, describing her heroine's proposed marriage as a "worse confinement" than the life of a nun. But in her most successful novel, *Oroonoko*, Aphra Behn assimilated her personal quarrels with the world into her larger concern with man's inhumanity to man.

Lore Metzger
EMORY UNIVERSITY

OROONOKO:

OR

THE HISTORY OF THE ROYAL SLAVE

I DO not pretend, in giving you the History of this
Royal Slave, to entertain my Reader with Adventures
of a feign'd *Hero*, whose Life and Fortunes Fancy may
manage at the Poet's pleasure; nor in relating the
Truth, design to adorn it with any Accidents, but such
as arrived in earnest to him: And it shall come simply
into the World, recommended by its own proper Merits,
and natural Intrigues; there being enough of Reality
to support it, and to render it diverting, without the
addition of Invention.

I was myself an Eye-witness to a great part of what
you will find here set down; and what I cou'd not be
Witness of, I receiv'd from the Mouth of the chief Actor
in this History, the *Hero* himself, who gave us the whole
Transactions of his Youth: And though I shall omit,
for brevity's sake, a thousand little Accidents of his
life, which, however pleasant to us, where History was
scarce, and Adventures very rare, yet might prove
tedious and heavy to my Reader, in a World where he
finds Diversions for every Minute, new and strange.
But we who were perfectly charm'd with the Character
of this great Man, were curious to gather every Circum-
stance of his Life.

The Scene of the last part of his Adventures lies in a
Colony in *America*, called *Surinam*, in the *West-Indies*.

But before I give you the Story of this *Gallant Slave*,
'tis fit I tell you the manner of bringing them to these
new *Colonies*; those they make use of there, not being
Natives of the place: for those we live with in perfect

1

Amity, without daring to command 'em; but, on the
contrary, caress 'em with all the brotherly and friendly
Affection in the world; trading with them for their
Fish, Venison, Buffalo's Skins, and little Rarities; as
Marmosets, a sort of Monkey, as big as a Rat or Weasel,
but of a marvellous and delicate shape, having Face
and Hands like a Human Creature; and *Cousheries*, a
little Beast in the form and fashion of a Lion, as big as
a Kitten, but so exactly made in all parts like that
Noble Beast, that it is it in *Miniature*. Then for little
Paraketoes, great *Parrots*, *Muckaws*, and a thousand
other Birds and Beasts of wonderful and surprizing
Forms, Shapes, and Colours. For Skins of prodigious
Snakes, of which there are some threescore Yards in
length; as is the Skin of one that may be seen at his
Majesty's *Antiquary's*; where are also some rare Flies,
of amazing Forms and Colours, presented to 'em by my
self; some as big as my Fist, some less; and all of
various Excellencies, such as Art cannot imitate. Then
we trade for Feathers, which they order into all
Shapes, make themselves little short Habits of 'em, and
glorious Wreaths for their Heads, Necks, Arms and
Legs, whose Tinctures are unconceivable. I had a Set
of these presented to me, and I gave 'em to the King's
Theatre, and it was the Dress of the *Indian Queen*,
infinitely admir'd by Persons of Quality; and was
unimitable. Besides these, a thousand little Knacks,
and Rarities in Nature; and some of Art, as their
Baskets, Weapons, Aprons, &c. We dealt with 'em
with Beads of all Colours, Knives, Axes, Pins and
Needles; which they us'd only as Tools to drill Holes
with in their Ears, Noses and Lips, where they hang a
great many little things; as long Beads, bits of Tin,
Brass or Silver beat thin, and any shining Trinket.
The Beads they weave into Aprons about a Quarter of
an Ell long, and of the same breadth; working them
very prettily in Flowers of several Colours; which Apron
they wear just before 'em, as *Adam* and *Eve* did the
Fig-leaves; the Men wearing a long stripe of Linen,

2

which they deal with us for. They thread these Beads
also on long Cotton-threads, and make Girdles to tie
their Aprons to, which come twenty times, or more,
about the Waste, and then cross, like a Shoulder - belt,
both ways, and round their Necks, Arms, and Legs.
This Adornment, with their long black Hair, and the
Face painted in little Specks or Flowers here and there,
makes 'em a wonderful Figure to behold. Some of the
Beauties, which indeed are finely shap'd, as almost all
are, and who have pretty Features, are charming and
novel; for they have all that is called Beauty, except
the Colour, which is a reddish Yellow; or after a new
Oiling, which they often use to themselves, they are of
the Colour of a new Brick, but smooth, soft and sleek.
They are extreme modest and bashful, very shy, and
nice of being touch'd. And though they are all thus
naked, if one lives for ever among 'em, there is not to
be seen an undecent Action, or Glance: and being continually us'd to see one another so unadorn'd, so like
our first Parents before the Fall, it seems as if they had
no Wishes, there being nothing to heighten Curiosity;
but all you can see, you see at once, and every moment
see; and where there is no Novelty, there can be no
Curiosity. Not but I have seen a handsome young
Indian, dying for Love of a very beautiful young *Indian*
Maid; but all his Courtship was, to fold his Arms, pursue
her with his Eyes, and Sighs were all his Language:
While she, as if no such Lover were present, or rather
as if she desired none such, carefully guarded her Eyes
from beholding him; and never approach'd him, but she
look'd down with all the blushing Modesty I have seen
in the most severe and cautious of our World. And
these People represented to me an absolute *Idea* of the
first State of Innocence, before *Man* knew how to sin:
And 'tis most evident and plain, that simple Nature is
the most harmless, inoffensive and vertuous Mistress.
'Tis she alone, if she were permitted, that better instructs
the World, than all the Inventions of Man: Religion
wou'd here but destroy that Tranquillity they possess

by Ignorance; and Laws wou'd but teach 'em to know Offence, of which now they have no Notion. They once made mourning and fasting for the Death of the *English* Governor, who had given his Hand to come on such a day to 'em, and neither came nor sent; believing, when a Man's word was past, nothing but Death cou'd or shou'd prevent his keeping it: And when they saw he was not dead, they ask'd him what Name they had for a Man who promis'd a thing he did not do? The Governor told them, Such a Man was a *Lyar*, which was a Word of Infamy to a Gentleman. Then one of 'em reply'd, *Governor, you are a Lyar, and guilty of that Infamy.* They have a native Justice, which knows no Fraud; and they understand no Vice, or Cunning, but when they are taught by the *White* Men. They have Plurality of Wives; which, when they grow old, serve those that succeed 'em, who are young, but with a Servitude easy and respected; and unless they take Slaves in War, they have no other Attendants.

Those on that *Continent* where I was, had no King; but the oldest War-Captain was obey'd with great Resignation.

A War-Captain is a Man who has led them on to Battle with Conduct and Success; of whom I shall have occasion to speak more hereafter, and of some other of their Customs and Manners, as they fall in my way.

With these People, as I said, we live in perfect Tranquillity, and good Understanding, as it behoves us to do; they knowing all the places where to seek the best Food of the Country, and the means of getting it; and for very small and unvaluable Trifles, supply us with that 'tis impossible for us to get: for they do not only in the Woods, and over the *Sevana's*, in Hunting, supply the parts of Hounds, by swiftly scouring through those almost impassable Places, and by the mere Activity of their Feet run down the nimblest Deer, and other eatable Beasts; but in the Water, one wou'd think they were Gods of the Rivers, or Fellow-Citizens of the deep; so rare an Art they have in swimming,

4

diving, and almost living in Water; by which they command the less swift Inhabitants of the Floods. And then for shooting, what they cannot take, or reach with their Hands, they do with Arrows; and have so admirable an Aim, that they will split almost an Hair, and at any distance that an Arrow can reach: they will shoot down Oranges, and other Fruit, and only touch the Stalk with the Dart's Point, that they may not hurt the Fruit. So that they being on all occasions very useful to us, we find it absolutely necessary to caress 'em as Friends, and not to treat 'em as Slaves, nor dare we do other, their numbers so far surpassing ours in that Continent.

Those then whom we make use of to work in our Plantations of Sugar, are *Negroes,* Black-Slaves all together, who are transported thither in this manner.

Those who want Slaves, make a Bargain with a Master, or a Captain of a Ship, and contract to pay him so much a-piece, a matter of twenty Pound a head, for as many as he agrees for, and to pay for 'em when they shall be deliver'd on such a Plantation: So that when there arrives a Ship laden with Slaves, they who have so contracted, go a-board, and receive their number by Lot; and perhaps in one Lot that may be for ten, there may happen to be three or four Men, the rest Women and Children. Or be there more or less of either Sex, you are obliged to be contented with your Lot.

Coramantien, a Country of *Blacks* so called, was one of those Places in which they found the most advantageous Trading for these Slaves, and thither most of our great Traders in that Merchandize traffick; for that Nation is very warlike and brave: and having a continual Campaign, being always in hostility with one neighbouring Prince or other, they had the fortune to take a great many Captives: for all they took in Battle were sold as Slaves; at least those common Men who cou'd not ransom themselves. Of these Slaves so taken, the General only has all the Profit; and of these

Generals our Captains and Masters of Ships buy all their Freights.

The King of *Coramantien* was himself a Man of an hundred and odd Years old, and had no Son, tho he had many beautiful Black Wives: for most certainly there are Beauties that can charm of that Colour. In his younger Years he had had many gallant Men to his Sons, thirteen of whom died in Battle, conquering when they fell; and he had only left him for his Successor, one Grand-child, Son to one of these dead Victors, who, as soon as he could bear a Bow in his Hand, and a Quiver at his Back, was sent into the Field to be train'd up by one of the oldest Generals to War; where, from his natural Inclination to Arms, and the Occasions given him, with the good Conduct of the old General, he became, at the Age of seventeen, one of the most expert Captains, and bravest Soldiers that ever saw the Field of *Mars*: so that he was ador'd as the wonder of all that World, and the Darling of the Soldiers. Besides, he was adorn'd with a native Beauty, so transcending all those of his gloomy Race, that he struck an Awe and Reverence, even into those that knew not his Quality; as he did into me, who beheld him with surprize and wonder, when afterwards he arrived in our World.

He had scarce arrived at his seventeenth Year, when, fighting by his side, the General was kill'd with an Arrow in his Eye, which the Prince *Oroonoko* (for so was this gallant *Moor* call'd) very narrowly avoided; nor had he, if the General who saw the Arrow shot, and perceiving it aimed at the Prince, had not bow'd his Head between, on purpose to receive it in his own Body, rather than it should touch that of the Prince, and so saved him.

'Twas then, afflicted as *Oroonoko* was, that he was proclaimed General in the old Man's place: and then it was, at the finishing of that War, which had continu'd for two Years, that the Prince came to Court, where he had hardly been a Month together, from the time of his fifth Year to that of seventeen; and 'twas amazing to imagine where it was he learn'd so much Humanity: or, to give his Accomplishments a juster Name, where 'twas he got that real Greatness of Soul, those refined Notions of true Honour, that absolute Generosity, and that Softness that was capable of the highest Passions of Love and Gallantry, whose Objects were almost continually fighting Men, or those mangled or dead, who heard no Sounds but those of War and Groans. Some part of it we may attribute to the care of a *Frenchman* of Wit and Learning, who finding it turn to very good account to be a sort of Royal Tutor to this young Black, and perceiving him very ready, apt, and quick of Apprehension, took a great pleasure to teach him Morals, Language and Science; and was for it extremely belov'd and valu'd by him. Another Reason was, he lov'd when he came from War, to see all the *English* Gentlemen that traded thither; and did not only learn their Language, but that of the *Spaniard* also, with whom he traded afterwards for Slaves.

I have often seen and conversed with this Great Man, and been a Witness to many of his mighty Actions; and do assure my Reader, the most illustrious Courts could not have produced a braver Man, both for Greatness of Courage and Mind, a Judgment more solid, a Wit more quick, and a Conversation more sweet and diverting. He knew almost as much as if he had read much: He had heard of and admired the *Romans*: He had heard of the late Civil Wars in *England*, and the deplorable Death of our great Monarch; and wou'd discourse of it with all the Sense and Abhorrence of the Injustice imaginable. He had an extreme good and graceful Mien, and all the Civility of a well-bred great Man. He had nothing of Barbarity in his Nature, but in all Points address'd himself as if his Education had been in some *European* Court.

This great and just Character of *Oroonoko* gave me an extreme Curiosity to see him, especially when I knew he spoke *French* and *English*, and that I could talk with

7

him. But though I had heard so much of him, I was
as greatly surprized when I saw him, as if I had heard
nothing of him; so beyond all Report I found him. He
came into the Room, and addressed himself to me, and
some other Women, with the best Grace in the World.
He was pretty tall, but of a Shape the most exact that
can be fancy'd: The most famous Statuary cou'd not
form the Figure of a Man more admirably turn'd from
head to foot. His Face was not of that brown rusty
Black which most of that Nation are, but of perfect
Ebony, or polished Jett. His Eyes were the most awful
that cou'd be seen, and very piercing; the White of
'em being like Snow, as were his Teeth. His Nose was
rising and *Roman*, instead of *African* and flat. His
Mouth the finest shaped that could be seen; far from
those great turn'd Lips, which are so natural to the
rest of the Negroes. The whole Proportion and Air of
his Face was so nobly and exactly form'd, that bating
his Colour, there could be nothing in Nature more
beautiful, agreeable and handsome. There was no one
Grace wanting, that bears the Standard of true Beauty.
His Hair came down to his Shoulders, by the Aids of
Art, which was by pulling it out with a Quill, and
keeping it comb'd; of which he took particular care.
Nor did the Perfections of his Mind come short of those
of his Person; for his Discourse was admirable upon
almost any Subject: and whoever had heard him speak,
wou'd have been convinced of their Errors, that all
fine Wit is confined to the white Men, especially to
those of Christendom; and wou'd have confess'd that
Oroonoko was as capable even of reigning well, and
of governing as wisely, had as great a Soul, as politick
Maxims, and was as sensible of Power, as any Prince
civiliz'd in the most refined Schools of Humanity and
Learning, or the most illustrious Courts.

This Prince, such as I have describ'd him, whose
Soul and Body were so admirably adorned, was (while
yet he was in the Court of his Grandfather, as I said)
as capable of Love, as 'twas possible for a brave and

gallant Man to be; and in saying that, I have named the highest Degree of Love: for sure great Souls are most capable of that Passion.

I have already said, the old General was kill'd by the Shot of an Arrow by the side of this Prince in Battle; and that *Oroonoko* was made General. This old dead Hero had one only Daughter left of his Race, a Beauty, that to describe her truly, one need say only, she was Female to the noble Male; the beautiful Black *Venus* to our young *Mars*; as charming in her Person as he, and of delicate Vertues. I have seen a hundred White men sighing after her, and making a thousand Vows at her feet, all in vain, and unsuccessful. And she was indeed too great for any but a Prince of her own Nation to adore.

Oroonoko coming from the Wars (which were now ended) after he had made his Court to his Grandfather, he thought in honour he ought to make a Visit to *Imoinda*, the Daughter of his Foster-father, the dead General; and to make some Excuses to her, because his Preservation was the occasion of her Father's Death; and to present her with those Slaves that had been taken in this last Battle, as the Trophies of her Father's Victories. When he came, attended by all the young Soldiers of any Merit, he was infinitely surpriz'd at the Beauty of this fair Queen of Night, whose Face and Person was so exceeding all he had ever beheld, that lovely Modesty with which she receiv'd him, that Softness in her Look and Sighs, upon the melancholy Occasion of this Honour that was done by so great a Man as *Oroonoko*, and a Prince of whom she had heard such admirable things; the Awfulness wherewith she receiv'd him, and the Sweetness of her Words and Behaviour while he stay'd, gain'd a perfect Conquest over his fierce Heart, and made him feel, the Victor cou'd be subdu'd. So that having made his first Compliments, and presented her an hundred and fifty Slaves in Fetters, he told her with his Eyes, that he was not insensible of her Charms; while *Imoinda*, who wish'd

9

for nothing more than so glorious a Conquest, was pleas'd to believe, she understood that silent Language of new-born Love; and, from that moment, put on all her additions to Beauty.

The Prince return'd to Court with quite another Humour than before; and though he did not speak much of the fair *Imoinda*, he had the pleasure to hear all his Followers speak of nothing but the Charms of that Maid, insomuch that, even in the presence of the old King, they were extolling her, and heightning, if possible, the Beauties they had found in her: so that nothing else was talk'd of, no other Sound was heard in every Corner where there were Whisperers, but *Imoinda! Imoinda!*

'Twill be imagin'd *Oroonoko* stay'd not long before he made his second Visit; nor, considering his Quality, not much longer before he told her, he ador'd her. I have often heard him say, that he admir'd by what strange Inspiration he came to talk things so soft, and so passionate, who never knew Love, nor was us'd to the Conversation of Women; but (to use his own words) he said, Most happily, some new, and, till then, unknown Power instructed his Heart and Tongue in the Language of Love, and at the same time, in favour of him, inspir'd *Imoinda* with a sense of his Passion. She was touch'd with what he said, and return'd it all in such Answers as went to his very Heart, with a Pleasure unknown before. Nor did he use those Obligations ill, that Love had done him. but turn'd all his happy moments to the best advantage; and as he knew no Vice, his Flame aim'd at nothing but Honour, if such a distinction may be made in Love; and especially in that Country, where Men take to themselves as many as they can maintain; and where the only Crime and Sin with Woman, is, to turn her off, to abandon her to want, shame and misery: such ill Morals are only practis'd in *Christian* Countries, where they prefer the bare Name of Religion; and, without Vertue or Morality. think that sufficient. But *Oroonoko* was none of those

10

Professors; but as he had right Notions of Honour, so
he made her such Propositions as were not only and
barely such; but, contrary to the custom of his Country,
he made her Vows, she shou'd be the only Woman he
wou'd possess while he liv'd; that no Age or Wrinkles
shou'd encline him to change; for her Soul wou'd be
always fine, and always young; and he shou'd have an
eternal *Idea* in his Mind of the Charms she now bore;
and shou'd look into his Heart for that *Idea*, when he
cou'd find it no longer in her Face.

After a thousand Assurances of his lasting Flame,
and her eternal Empire over him, she condescended to
receive him for her Husband; or rather, receiv'd him,
as the greatest Honour the Gods cou'd do her.

There is a certain Ceremony in these cases to be
observ'd, which I forgot to ask how 'twas perform'd;
but 'twas concluded on both sides, that in obedience to
him, the Grandfather was to be first made acquainted
with the Design: For they pay a most absolute Resignation to the Monarch, especially when he is a Parent also.

On the other side, the old King, who had many Wives,
and many Concubines, wanted not Court-Flatterers to
insinuate into his Heart a thousand tender Thoughts
for this young Beauty; and who represented her to his
Fancy, as the most charming he had ever possess'd
in all the long race of his numerous Years. At this
Character, his old Heart, like an extinguish'd Brand,
most apt to take fire, felt new Sparks of Love, and
began to kindle; and now grown to his second Childhood, long'd with impatience to behold this gay thing,
with whom, alas! he could but innocently play. But
how he shou'd be confirm'd she was this *Wonder*, before
he us'd his Power to call her to Court, (where Maidens
never came, unless for the King's private Use) he was
next to consider; and while he was so doing, he had
Intelligence brought him, that *Imoinda* was most certainly Mistress to the Prince *Oroonoko*. This gave him
some *Chagreen*: however, it gave him also an opportunity, one day, when the Prince was a hunting, to wait

on a Man of Quality, as his Slave and Attendant, who should go and make a Present to *Imoinda*, as from the Prince; he should then, unknown, see this fair Maid, and have an opportunity to hear what Message she wou'd return the Prince for his Present, and from thence gather the state of her Heart, and degree of her Inclination. This was put in execution, and the old Monarch saw, and burn'd: He found her all he had heard, and would not delay his Happiness, but found he should have some Obstacle to overcome her Heart; for she express'd her sense of the Present the Prince had sent her, in terms so sweet, so soft and pretty, with an Air of Love and Joy that cou'd not be dissembled, insomuch that 'twas past doubt whether she lov'd *Oroonoko* entirely. This gave the old King some affliction; but he salv'd it with this, that the Obedience the People pay their King, was not at all inferiour to what they paid their Gods; and what Love wou'd not oblige *Imoinda* to do, Duty wou'd compel her to.

He was therefore no sooner got to his Apartment, but he sent the Royal Veil to *Imoinda*; that is, the Ceremony of Invitation: He sends the Lady he has a mind to honour with his Bed, a Veil, with which she is cover'd, and secur'd for the King's Use; and 'tis Death to disobey; besides, held a most impious Disobedience.

'Tis not to be imagin'd the Surprize and Grief that seiz'd the lovely Maid at this News and Sight. However, as Delays in these cases are dangerous, and Pleading worse than Treason; trembling, and almost fainting, she was oblig'd to suffer her self to be cover'd, and led away.

They brought her thus to Court; ánd the King, who had caus'd a very rich Bath to be prepar'd, was led into it, where he sate under a Canopy, in State, to receive this long'd-for Virgin; whom he having commanded shou'd be brought to him, they (after disrobing her) led her to the Bath, and making fast the Doors, left her to descend. The King, without more Courtship, bad her throw off her Mantle, and come to his

Arms. But *Imoinda*, all in Tears, threw her self on the Marble, on the brink of the Bath, and besought him to hear her. She told him, as she was a Maid, how proud of the Divine Glory she should have been, of having it in her power to oblige her King; but as by the Laws he could not, and from his Royal Goodness would not take from any Man his wedded Wife; so she believ'd she shou'd be the Occasion of making him commit a great Sin, if she did not reveal her State and Condition; and tell him, she was another's, and cou'd not be so happy to be his.

The King, enrag'd at this Delay, hastily demanded the Name of the bold Man, that had married a Woman of her Degree, without his Consent. *Imoinda*, seeing his Eyes fierce, and his Hands tremble, (whether with Age or Anger, I know not, but she fancy'd the last) almost repented she had said so much, for now she fear'd the storm wou'd fall on the Prince; she therefore said a thousand things to appease the raging of his Flame, and to prepare him to hear who it was with calmness: but before she spoke, he imagin'd who she meant, but wou'd not seem to do so, but commanded her to lay aside her Mantle, and suffer her self to receive his Caresses, or, by his Gods he swore, that happy Man whom she was going to name shou'd die, though it were even *Oroonoko* himself. *Therefore* (said he) *deny this Marriage, and swear thy self a Maid.* That (reply'd *Imoinda*) *by all our Powers I do ; for I am not yet known to my Husband.* 'Tis enough (said the King;) *'tis enough both to satisfy my Conscience, and my Heart.* And rising from his Seat, he went and led her into the Bath; it being in vain for her to resist.

In this time, the Prince, who was return'd from Hunting, went to visit his *Imoinda*, but found her gone; and not only so, but heard she had receiv'd the Royal Veil. This rais'd him to a storm; and in his madness, they had much ado to save him from laying violent hands on himself. Force first prevail'd, and then Reason: They urg'd all to him, that might oppose his

Rage; but nothing weigh'd so greatly with him as the King's Old Age, uncapable of injuring him with *Imoinda*. He wou'd give way to that Hope, because it pleas'd him most, and flatter'd best his Heart. Yet this serv'd not altogether to make him cease his different Passions, which sometimes rag'd within him, and softned into Showers. 'Twas not enough to appease him, to tell him, his Grandfather was old, and cou'd not that way injure him, while he retain'd that awful Duty which the young Men are us'd there to pay to their grave Relations. He cou'd not be convinc'd he had no cause to sigh and mourn for the loss of a Mistress, he cou'd not with all his strength and courage retrieve. And he wou'd often cry, *Oh, my Friends ! were she in wall'd Cities, or confin'd from me in Fortifications of the greatest strength ; did Inchantments or Monsters detain her from me ; I wou'd venture through any Hazard to free her : But here, in the Arms of a feeble Old Man, my Youth, my violent Love, my Trade in Arms, and all my vast Desire of Glory, avail me nothing.* Imoinda *is as irrecoverably lost to me, as if she were snatch'd by the cold Arms of Death : Oh ! she is never to be retriev'd. If I wou'd wait tedious Years, till Fate shou'd bow the old King to his Grave, even that wou'd not leave me* Imoinda *free ; but still that Custom that makes it so vile a Crime for a Son to marry his Father's Wives or Mistresses, wou'd hinder my Happiness ; unless I wou'd either ignobly set an ill Precedent to my Successors, or abandon my Country, and fly with her to some unknown World who never heard our Story.*

But it was objected to him, That his Case was not the same; for *Imoinda* being his lawful Wife by solemn Contract, 'twas he was the injur'd Man, and might, if he so pleas'd, take *Imoinda* back, the breach of the Law being on his Grandfather's side; and that if he cou'd circumvent him, and redeem her from the *Otan*, which is the Palace of the King's Women, a sort of *Seraglio*, it was both just and lawful for him so to do. This Reasoning had some force upon him, and he shou'd have been entirely comforted, but for the thought that she was possess'd by his Grandfather. However, he lov'd so well, that he was resolv'd to believe what most favour'd his Hope, and to endeavour to learn from *Imoinda's* own mouth, what only she cou'd satisfy him in, whether she was robb'd of that Blessing which was only due to his Faith and Love. But as it was very hard to get a sight of the Women, (for no Men ever enter'd into the *Otan,* but when the King went to entertain himself with some one of his Wives or Mistresses; and 'twas Death, at any other time, for any other to go in) so he knew not how to contrive to get a sight of her.

While *Oroonoko* felt all the Agonies of Love, and suffer'd under a Torment the most painful in the World, the old King was not exempted from his share of Affliction. He was troubled, for having been forc'd, by an irresistible Passion, to rob his Son of a Treasure, he knew, cou'd not but be extremely dear to him; since she was the most beautiful that ever had been seen, and had besides, all the Sweetness and Innocence of Youth and Modesty, with a Charm of Wit surpassing all. He found, that however she was forc'd to expose her lovely Person to his wither'd Arms, she cou'd only sigh and weep there, and think of *Oroonoko;* and often-times cou'd not forbear speaking of him, tho her Life were, by Custom, forfeited by owning her Passion. But she spoke not of a Lover only, but of a Prince dear to him to whom she spoke; and of the Praises of a Man, who, till now, fill'd the old Man's Soul with Joy at every recital of his Bravery, or even his Name. And 'twas this Dotage on our young Hero, that gave *Imoinda* a thousand Privileges to speak of him, without offending; and this Condescension in the old King, that made her take the Satisfaction of speaking of him so very often.

Besides, he many times enquir'd how the Prince bore himself: And those of whom he ask'd, being entirely Slaves to the Merits and Vertues of the Prince, still answer'd what they thought conduc'd best to his

Service; which was, to make the old King fancy that the Prince had no more Interest in *Imoinda*, and had resign'd her willingly to the Pleasure of the King; that he diverted himself with his Mathematicians, his Fortifications, his Officers, and his Hunting.

This pleas'd the old Lover, who fail'd not to report these things again to *Imoinda*, that she might, by the Example of her young Lover, withdraw her Heart, and rest better contented in his Arms. But, however she was forc'd to receive this unwelcome News, in all appearance, with unconcern and content; her Heart was bursting within, and she was only happy when she cou'd get alone, to vent her Griefs and Moans with Sighs and Tears.

What Reports of the Prince's Conduct were made to the King, he thought good to justify as far as possibly he cou'd by his Actions; and when he appear'd in the Presence of the King, he shew'd a Face not at all betraying his Heart: so that in a little time, the old Man, being entirely convinc'd that he was no longer a Lover of *Imoinda*, he carry'd him with him, in his Train, to the *Otan*, often to banquet with his Mistresses. But as soon as he enter'd, one day, into the Apartment of *Imoinda*, with the King, at the first Glance from her Eyes, notwithstanding all his determined Resolution, he was ready to sink in the place where he stood; and had certainly done so, but for the support of *Aboan*, a young Man who was next to him; which, with his Change of Countenance, had betray'd him, had the King chanc'd to look that way. And I have observ'd, 'tis a very great Error in those who laugh when one says, *A* Negro *can change Colour*: for I have seen 'em as frequently blush, and look pale, and that as visibly as ever I saw in the most beautiful *White*. And 'tis certain, that both these Changes were evident, this day, in both these Lovers. And *Imoinda*, who saw with some Joy the Change in the Prince's Face, and found it in her own, strove to divert the King from beholding either, by a forc'd Caress, with which she met him;

OROONOKO

which was a new Wound in the Heart of the poor dying
Prince. But as soon as the King was busy'd in looking
on some fine thing of *Imoinda's* making, she had time
to tell the Prince, with her angry, but Love-darting
Eyes, that she resented his Coldness, and bemoan'd
her own miserable Captivity. Nor were his Eyes silent,
but answer'd hers again, as much as Eyes cou'd do,
instructed by the most tender and most passionate
Heart that ever lov'd: And they spoke so well, and
so effectually, as *Imoinda* no longer doubted but she
was the only delight and darling of that Soul she found
pleading in 'em its right of Love, which none was more
willing to resign than she. And 'twas this powerful
Language alone that in an instant convey'd all the
Thoughts of their Souls to each other; that they both
found there wanted but Opportunity to make them
both entirely happy. But when he saw another Door
open'd by *Onahal* (a former old Wife of the King's, who
now had Charge of *Imoinda*,) and saw the Prospect of a
Bed of State made ready, with Sweets and Flowers for
the dalliance of the King, who immediately led the
trembling Victim from his sight, into that prepar'd
Repose; what Rage! what wild Frenzies seiz'd his Heart!
which forcing to keep within bounds, and to suffer without noise, it became the more insupportable, and rent
his Soul with ten thousand Pains. He was forced to
retire to vent his Groans, where he fell down on a
Carpet, and lay struggling a long time, and only breathing now and then—Oh *Imoinda*! When *Onahal* had
finished her necessary Affair within, shutting the Door,
she came forth, to wait till the King called; and hearing
some one sighing in the other Room, she past on, and
found the Prince in that deplorable Condition, which
she thought needed her Aid. She gave him Cordials,
but all in vain; till finding the Nature of his Disease,
by his Sighs, and naming *Imoinda*, she told him he had
not so much cause as he imagined to afflict himself: for
if he knew the King so well as she did, he wou'd not lose
a moment in Jealousy; and that she was confident

17

that *Imoinda* bore, at this minute, part in his Affliction. *Aboan* was of the same opinion, and both together persuaded him to re-assume his Courage; and all sitting down on the Carpet, the Prince said so many obliging things to *Onahal*, that he half-persuaded her to be of his Party: and she promised him, she would thus far comply with his just Desires, that she would let *Imoinda* know how faithful he was, what he suffer'd, and what he said.

This Discourse lasted till the King called, which gave *Oroonoko* a certain Satisfaction; and with the Hope *Onahal* had made him conceive, he assumed a Look as gay as 'twas possible a Man in his circumstances could do: and presently after, he was call'd in with the rest who waited without. The King commanded Musick to be brought, and several of his young Wives and Mistresses came all together by his Command, to dance before him; where *Imoinda* perform'd her Part with an Air and Grace so surpassing all the rest, as her Beauty was above 'em, and received the Present ordained as a Prize. The Prince was every moment more charmed with the new Beauties and Graces he beheld in this Fair-One; and while he gazed, and she danc'd, *Onahal* was retired to a Window with *Aboan*.

This *Onahal*, as I said, was one of the Cast-Mistresses of the old King; and 'twas these (now past their Beauty) that were made Guardians or Governantees to the new and the young ones, and whose business it was to teach them all those wanton Arts of Love, with which they prevail'd and charmed heretofore in their turn; and who now treated the triumphing Happy-ones with all the Severity as to Liberty and Freedom, that was possible, in revenge of their Honours they rob them of; envying them those Satisfactions, those Gallantries and Presents, that were once made to themselves, while Youth and Beauty lasted, and which they now saw pass, as it were regardless by, and paid only to the Bloomings. And certainly, nothing is more afflicting to a decay'd Beauty, than to behold in it self declining

Charms, that were once ador'd; and to find those
Caresses paid to new Beauties, to which once she laid
claim; to hear them whisper, as she passes by, that
once was a delicate Woman. Those abandon'd Ladies
therefore endeavour to revenge all the despights and
decays of time, on these flourishing Happy-ones. And
'twas this Severity that gave *Oroonoko* a thousand Fears
he should never prevail with *Onahal* to see *Imoinda*. But,
as I said, she was now retir'd to a Window with *Aboan*.

This young Man was not only one of the best Quality,
but a Man extremely well made, and beautiful; and
coming often to attend the King to the *Otan*, he had
subdu'd the Heart of the antiquated *Onahal*, which
had not forgot how pleasant it was to be in love. And
though she had some Decays in her Face, she had none
in her Sense and Wit; she was there agreeable still,
even to *Aboan's* Youth: so that he took pleasure in
entertaining her with Discourses of Love. He knew
also, that to make his court to these She-favourites,
was the way to be great; these being the Persons that
do all Affairs and Business at Court. He had also
observed that she had given him Glances more tender
and inviting than she had done to others of his Quality.
And now, when he saw that her Favour cou'd so absolutely oblige the Prince, he fail'd not to sigh in her
Ear, and to look with Eyes all soft upon her, and gave
her hope that she had made some Impressions on his
Heart. He found her pleas'd at this, and making a
thousand Advances to him: but the Ceremony ending,
and the King departing, broke up the Company for that
day, and his Conversation.

Aboan fail'd not that night to tell the Prince of his
Success, and how advantageous the Service of *Onahal*
might be to his Amour with *Imoinda*. The Prince was
over-joy'd with this good News, and besought him if it
were possible to caress her so, as to engage her entirely,
which he could not fail to do, if he comply'd with her
Desires: *For then* (said the Prince) *her Life lying at your
mercy, she must grant you the Request you make in my*

19

behalf. Aboan understood him, and assur'd him he would make love so effectually, that he would defy the most expert Mistress of the Art, to find out whether he dissembled it, or had it really. And 'twas with impatience they waited the next opportunity of going to the *Otan.*

The Wars came on, the time of taking the Field approached; and 'twas impossible for the Prince to delay his going at the Head of his Army to encounter the Enemy; so that every Day seem'd a tedious Year, till he saw his *Imoinda*: for he believed he cou'd not live, if he were forced away without being so happy. 'Twas with impatience therefore that he expected the next Visit the King wou'd make; and according to his Wish it was not long.

The Parley of the Eyes of these two Lovers had not pass'd so secretly, but an old jealous Lover could spy it; or rather, he wanted not Flatterers who told him they observ'd it: so that the Prince was hasten'd to the Camp, and this was the last Visit he found he should make to the *Otan*; he therefore urged *Aboan* to make the best of this last Effort, and to explain himself so to *Onahal*, that she deferring her Enjoyment of her young Lover no longer, might make way for the Prince to speak to *Imoinda.*

The whole Affair being agreed on between the Prince and *Aboan*, they attended the King, as the Custom was, to the *Otan*; where, while the whole Company was taken up in beholding the Dancing, and Antick Postures the Women-Royal made, to divert the King, *Onahal* singled out *Aboan*, whom she found most pliable to her wish. When she had him where she believ'd she cou'd not be heard, she sigh'd to him, and softly cry'd, *Ah*, Aboan *! when will you be sensible of my Passion ? I confess it with my Mouth, because I would not give my Eyes the Lye ; and you have but too much already perceived they have confess'd my Flame : nor would I have you believe, that because I am the abandoned Mistress of a King, I esteem my self altogether divested of Charms : No,* Aboan *;*

I have still a Rest of Beauty enough engaging, and have learn'd to please too well, not to be desirable. I can have Lovers still, but will have none but Aboan. *Madam,* (reply'd the half-feigning Youth) *you have already, by my Eyes, found you can still conquer ; and I believe 'tis in pity of me you condescend to this kind Confession. But, Madam, Words are used to be so small a part of our Country-Courtship, that 'tis rare one can get so happy an Opportunity as to tell one's Heart ; and those few Minutes we have, are forced to be snatch'd for more certain Proofs of Love than speaking and sighing ; and such I languish for.*

He spoke this with such a Tone, that she hoped it true, and cou'd not forbear believing it; and being wholly transported with Joy for having subdued the finest of all the King's Subjects to her Desires, she took from her Ears two large Pearls, and commanded him to wear 'em in his. He would have refused 'em, crying, *Madam, these are not the Proofs of your Love that I expect ; 'tis Opportunity, 'tis a Lone-Hour only, that can make me happy.* But forcing the Pearls into his Hand, she whisper'd softly to him; *Oh ! do not fear a Woman's Invention, when Love sets her a thinking.* And pressing his Hand, she cry'd, *This Night you shall be happy : Come to the Gate of the Orange-Grove, behind the* Otan, *and I will be ready about Mid-night to receive you.* 'Twas thus agreed, and she left him, that no notice might be taken of their speaking together.

The Ladies were still dancing, and the King laid on a Carpet with a great deal of Pleasure was beholding them, especially *Imoinda*, who that day appear'd more lovely than ever, being enliven'd with the good Tidings *Onahal* had brought her, of the constant Passion the Prince had for her. The Prince was laid on another Carpet at the other end of the Room, with his Eyes fixed on the Object of his Soul; and as she turned or moved, so did they: and she alone gave his Eyes and Soul their Motions. Nor did *Imoinda* employ her Eyes to any other use, than in beholding with infinite pleasure the Joy she produced in those of the Prince. But while she was more regarding him, than the Steps she took, she chanced to fall; and so near him, as that leaping with extreme force from the Carpet, he caught her in his Arms as she fell: and 'twas visible to the whole Presence, the Joy wherewith he received her. He clasped her close to his Bosom, and quite forgot that Reverence that was due to the Mistress of a King, and that Punishment that is the Reward of a Boldness of this nature. And had not the Presence of Mind of *Imoinda* (fonder of his Safety, than her own) befriended him, in making her spring from his Arms, and fall into her Dance again, he had at that instant met his Death; for the old King, jealous to the last degree, rose up in rage, broke all the Diversion, and led *Imoinda* to her Apartment, and sent out word to the Prince, to go immediately to the Camp; and that if he were found another Night in Court, he shou'd suffer the Death ordained for disobedient Offenders.

You may imagine how welcome this News was to *Oroonoko*, whose unseasonable Transport and Caress of *Imoinda* was blamed by all Men that loved him: and now he perceived his Fault, yet cry'd, *That for such another Moment he would be content to die.*

All the *Otan* was in disorder about this Accident; and *Onahal* was particularly concern'd, because on the Prince's Stay depended her Happiness; for she cou'd no longer expect that of *Aboan*: So that e'er they departed, they contrived it so, that the Prince and he should both come that night to the Grove of the *Otan*, which was all of Oranges and Citrons, and that there they wou'd wait her Orders.

They parted thus with Grief enough till night, leaving the King in possession of the lovely Maid. But nothing could appease the Jealousy of the old Lover; he wou'd not be imposed on, but would have it, that *Imoinda* made a false Step on purpose to fall into *Oroonoko's* Bosom, and that all things looked like a Design on both sides; and 'twas in vain she protested her Innocence:

He was old and obstinate, and left her more than half assur'd that his Fear was true.

The King going to his Apartment, sent to know where the Prince was, and if he intended to obey his Command. The Messenger return'd, and told him, he found the Prince pensive, and altogether unprepar'd for the Campaign; that he lay negligently on the ground, and answer'd very little. This confirmed the Jealousy of the King, and he commanded that they should very narrowly and privately watch his Motions; and that he should not stir from his Apartment, but one Spy or other shou'd be employ'd to watch him: So that the hour approaching, wherein he was to go to the Citron-Grove; and taking only *Aboan* along with him, he leaves his Apartment, and was watched to the very Gate of the *Otan*; where he was seen to enter, and where they left him, to carry back the Tidings to the King.

Oroonoko and *Aboan* were no sooner enter'd, but *Onahal* led the Prince to the Apartment of *Imoinda*; who, not knowing any thing of her Happiness, was laid in Bed. But *Onahal* only left him in her Chamber, to make the best of his Opportunity, and took her dear *Aboan* to her own; where he shew'd the height of Complaisance for his Prince, when, to give him an opportunity, he suffer'd himself to be caress'd in bed by *Onahal*.

The Prince softly waken'd *Imoinda*, who was not a little surpriz'd with Joy to find him there; and yet she trembled with a thousand Fears. I believe he omitted saying nothing to this young Maid, that might persuade her to suffer him to seize his own, and take the Rights of Love. And I believe she was not long resisting those Arms where she so long'd to be; and having Opportunity, Night, and Silence, Youth, Love and Desire, he soon prevail'd, and ravished in a moment what his old Grandfather had been endeavouring for so many Months.

'Tis not to be imagined the Satisfaction of these two young Lovers; nor the Vows she made him, that she remained a spotless Maid till that night, and that what she did with his Grandfather had robb'd him of no part of her Virgin-Honour; the Gods, in Mercy and Justice, having reserved that for her plighted Lord, to whom of right it belonged. And 'tis impossible to express the Transports he suffer'd, while he listen'd to a Discourse so charming from her loved Lips; and clasped that Body in his Arms, for whom he had so long languished: and nothing now afflicted him, but his sudden Departure from her; for he told her the Necessity, and his Commands, but should depart satisfy'd in this, That since the old King had hitherto not been able to deprive him of those Enjoyments which only belonged to him, he believed for the future he would be less able to injure him: so that, abating the Scandal of the Veil, which was no otherwise so, than that she was Wife to another, he believed her safe, even in the Arms of the King, and innocent; yet would he have ventur'd at the Conquest of the World, and have given it all to have had her avoided that Honour of receiving the *Royal Veil.* 'Twas thus, between a thousand Caresses, that both bemoan'd the hard Fate of Youth and Beauty, so liable to that cruel Promotion: 'twas a Glory that could well have been spared here, tho desired and aim'd at by all the young Females of that Kingdom.

But while they were thus fondly employ'd, forgetting how time ran on, and that the Dawn must conduct him far away from his only Happiness, they heard a great Noise in the *Otan*, and unusual Voices of Men; at which the Prince, starting from the Arms of the frighted *Imoinda*, ran to a little Battle-Ax he used to wear by his side; and having not so much leisure as to put on his Habit, he opposed himself against some who were already opening the Door: which they did with so much Violence, that *Oroonoko* was not able to defend it; but was forced to cry out with a commanding Voice, *Whoever ye are that have the Boldness to attempt to approach this Apartment thus rudely ; know, that I, the Prince* Oroonoko, *will revenge it with the certain Death of him that first enters : Therefore, stand back, and know, this Place is sacred to Love and Me this night ; to-morrow 'tis the King's.*

This he spoke with a Voice so resolv'd and assur'd, that they soon retired from the Door; but cry'd, *'Tis by the King's Command we are come ; and being satisfy'd by thy Voice, O Prince, as much as if we had enter'd, we can report to the King the Truth of all his Fears, and leave thee to provide for thy own Safety, as thou art advis'd by thy Friends.*

At these words they departed, and left the Prince to take a short and sad leave of his *Imoinda*; who, trusting in the Strength of her Charms, believed she should appease the Fury of a jealous King, by saying, she was surprized, and that it was by force of Arms he got into her Apartment. All her Concern now was for his Life, and therefore she hasten'd him to the Camp, and with much ado prevail'd on him to go. Nor was it she alone that prevailed; *Aboan* and *Onahal* both pleaded, and both assured him of a Lye that should be well enough contrived to secure *Imoinda*. So that at last, with a Heart sad as Death, dying Eyes, and sighing Soul, *Oroonoko* departed, and took his way to the Camp.

It was not long after, the King in Person came to the *Otan*; where beholding *Imoinda*, with Rage in his Eyes, he upbraided her Wickedness, and Perfidy; and threatning her Royal Lover, she fell on her face at his feet, bedewing the Floor with her Tears, and imploring his pardon for a Fault which she had not with her Will committed; as *Onahal*, who was also prostrate with her, could testify: That, unknown to her, he had broke into her Apartment, and ravished her. She spoke this much against her Conscience; but to save her own Life, 'twas absolutely necessary she should feign this Falsity. She knew it could not injure the Prince, he being fled to an Army that would stand by him, against any Injuries that should assault him. However this last Thought of *Imoinda's* being ravished, changed the

Measures of his Revenge; and whereas before he designed to be himself her Executioner, he now resolved she should not die. But as it is the greatest Crime in nature amongst 'em, to touch a Woman after having been possess'd by a Son, a Father, or a Brother, so now he looked on *Imoinda* as a polluted thing, wholly unfit for his Embrace; nor wou'd he resign her to his Grandson, because she had received the *Royal Veil*: He therefore removes her from the *Otan*, with *Onahal*; whom he put into safe hands, with order they should be both sold off as Slaves to another Country, either Christian or Heathen, 'twas no matter where.

This cruel Sentence, worse than Death, they implor'd might be reversed; but their Prayers were vain, and it was put in execution accordingly, and that with so much Secrecy, that none, either without or within the *Otan*, knew any thing of their Absence. or their Destiny.

The old King nevertheless executed this with a great deal of Reluctancy; but he believed he had made a very great Conquest over himself, when he had once resolved, and had perform'd what he resolv'd. He believed now, that his Love had been unjust; and that he cou'd not expect the Gods, or *Captain of the Clouds* (as they call the unknown Power) wou'd suffer a better Consequence from so ill a Cause. He now begins to hold *Oroonoko* excused; and to say, he had reason for what he did: And now every body cou'd assure the King how passionately *Imoinda* was beloved by the Prince; even those confess'd it now, who said the contrary before his Flame was not abated. So that the King being old, and not able to defend himself in War, and having no Sons of all his Race remaining alive, but only this, to maintain him on his Throne; and looking on this as a Man disobliged, first by the Rape of his Mistress, or rather Wife, and now by depriving him wholly of her, he fear'd, might make him desperate, and do some cruel thing, either to himself or his old Grandfather the Offender, he began to repent him extremely of the Contempt he had, in his Rage, put on *Imoinda*. Besides he consider'd he ought in honour to have killed her for this Offence, if it had been one. He ought to have had so much Value and Consideration for a Maid of her Quality, as to have nobly put her to death, and not to have sold her like a common Slave; the greatest Revenge, and the most disgraceful of any, and to which they a thousand times prefer Death, and implore it; as *Imoinda* did, but cou'd not obtain that Honour. Seeing therefore it was certain that *Oroonoko* would highly resent this Affront, he thought good to make some Excuse for his Rashness to him; and to that end, he sent a Messenger to the Camp, with Orders to treat with him about the Matter, to gain his Pardon, and to endeavour to mitigate his Grief; but that by no means he shou'd tell him she was sold, but secretly put to death: for he knew he should never obtain his Pardon for the other.

When the Messenger came, he found the Prince upon the point of engaging with the Enemy; but as soon as he heard of the arrival of the Messenger, he commanded him to his Tent, where he embraced him, and received him with Joy: which was soon abated by the down-cast Looks of the Messenger, who was instantly demanded the Cause by *Oroonoko*; who, impatient of delay, ask'd a thousand Questions in a breath, and all concerning *Imoinda*. But there needed little return; for he cou'd almost answer himself of all he demanded from his Sighs and Eyes. At last the Messenger casting himself at the Prince's feet, and kissing them with all the Submission of a Man that had something to implore which he dreaded to utter, he besought him to hear with Calmness what he had to deliver to him, and to call up all his noble and heroick Courage, to encounter with his Words, and defend himself against the ungrateful things he must relate. *Oroonoko* reply'd, with a deep Sigh, and a languishing Voice,—*I am armed against their worst Efforts—For I know they will tell me,* Imoinda *is no more—and after that, you may spare the rest.* Then, commanding him to rise, he laid himself on a Carpet, under a rich Pavilion, and remained a good while silent, and was hardly heard to sigh. When he was come a little to himself, the Messenger asked him leave to deliver that part of his Embassy which the Prince had not yet divin'd: And the Prince cry'd, *I permit thee*——Then he told him the Affliction the old King was in, for the Rashness he had committed in his Cruelty to *Imoinda*; and how he deign'd to ask pardon for his Offence, and to implore the Prince would not suffer that Loss to touch his Heart too sensibly, which now all the Gods cou'd not restore him, but might recompense him in Glory, which he begged he would pursue; and that Death, that common Revenger of all Injuries, would soon even the Account between him and a feeble old Man.

Oroonoko bad him return his Duty to his Lord and Master; and to assure him, there was no Account of Revenge to be adjusted between them: if there were, 'twas he was the Aggressor, and that Death would be just, and, maugre his Age, wou'd see him righted; and he was contented to leave his Share of Glory to Youths more fortunate and worthy of that Favour from the Gods: That henceforth he would never lift a Weapon, or draw a Bow, but abandon the small Remains of his Life to Sighs and Tears, and the continual Thoughts of what his Lord and Grandfather had thought good to send out of the World, with all that Youth, that Innocence and Beauty.

After having spoken this, whatever his greatest Officers and Men of the best Rank cou'd do, they could not raise him from the Carpet, or persuade him to Action, and Resolutions of Life; but commanding all to retire, he shut himself into his Pavilion all that day, while the Enemy was ready to engage: and wondring at the delay, the whole Body of the chief of the Army then address'd themselves to him, and to whom they had much ado to get Admittance. They fell on their faces at the foot of his Carpet, where they lay, and besought him with earnest Prayers and Tears, to lead them forth to Battle, and not let the Enemy take

Advantages of them; and implored him to have regard to his Glory, and to the World, that depended on his Courage and Conduct. But he made no other Reply to all their Supplications, but this, That he had now no more business for Glory; and for the World, it was a Trifle not worth his Care: *Go* (continued he, sighing) *and divide it amongst you, and reap with Joy what you so vainly prize, and leave me to my more welcome Destiny.*

They then demanded what they should do, and whom he would constitute in his room, that the Confusion of ambitious Youth and Power might not ruin their Order, and make them a Prey to the Enemy. He reply'd, he would not give himself the trouble—but wished 'em to chuse the bravest Man amongst 'em, let his Quality or Birth be what it wou'd: *For, Oh my Friends !* (said he) *it is not Titles make Men brave or good ; or Birth that bestows Courage and Generosity, or makes the Owner happy. Believe this, when you behold* Oroonoko *the most wretched, and abandoned by Fortune, of all the Creation of the Gods.* So turning himself about, he wou'd make no more Reply to all they could urge or implore.

The Army beholding their Officers return unsuccessful, with sad Faces and ominous Looks, that presaged no good luck, suffer'd a thousand Fears to take possession of their Hearts, and the Enemy to come even upon them, before they would provide for their Safety, by any Defence: and though they were assured by some, who had a mind to animate them, that they should be immediately headed by the Prince, and that in the mean time *Aboan* had orders to command as General; yet they were so dismay'd for want of that great Example of Bravery, that they could make but a very feeble Resistance; and at last, downright fled before the Enemy, who pursued 'em to the very Tents, killing 'em. Nor could all *Aboan's* Courage, which that day gained him immortal Glory. shame 'em into a manly Defence of themselves. The Guards that were left behind about the Prince's Tent, seeing the Soldiers flee before the Enemy, and scatter themselves all over the Plain, in

great disorder, made such out-cries as rouz'd the Prince
from his amorous Slumber, in which he had remain'd
bury'd for two days, without permitting any Sustenance
to approach him.   But, in spight of all his Resolutions,
he had not the Constancy of Grief to that degree, as to
make him insensible of the Danger of his Army; and in
that instant he leaped from his Couch, and cry'd—*Come,
if we must die, let us meet Death the noblest way ; and 'twill
be more like* Oroonoko *to encounter him at an Army's
Head, opposing the Torrent of a conquering Foe, than
lazily on a Couch, to wait his lingring Pleasure, and die
every moment by a thousand racking Thoughts ; or be
tamely taken by an Enemy, and led a whining love-sick
Slave to adorn the Triumphs of* Jamoan, *that young
Victor, who already is enter'd beyond the Limits I have
prescrib'd him.*

While he was speaking, he suffer'd his People to
dress him for the Field; and sallying out of his Pavilion,
with more Life and Vigour in his Countenance than
ever he shew'd, he appear'd like some Divine Power
descended to save his Country from Destruction: and
his People had purposely put him on all things that
might make him shine with most Splendor, to strike a
reverend Awe into the Beholders.   He flew into the
thickest of those that were pursuing his Men; and being
animated with Despair, he fought as if he came on
purpose to die, and did such things as will not be
believed that Human Strength could perform; and such
as soon inspir'd all the rest with new Courage, and
new Order.   And now it was that they began to fight
indeed; and so, as if they would not be outdone even by
their ador'd Hero; who turning the Tide of the Victory,
changing absolutely the Fate of the Day, gain'd an
entire Conquest: and *Oroonoko* having the good Fortune
to single out *Jamoan*, he took him prisoner with his
own Hand, having wounded him almost to death.

This *Jamoan* afterwards became very dear to him,
being a Man very gallant, and of excellent Graces, and
fine Parts; so that he never put him amongst the Rank

of Captives, as they used to do, without distinction, for the common Sale, or Market, but kept him in his own Court, where he retain'd nothing of the Prisoner but the Name, and returned no more into his own Country; so great an Affection he took for *Oroonoko*, and by a thousand Tales and Adventures of Love and Gallantry, flatter'd his Disease of Melancholy and Languishment: which I have often heard him say, had certainly kill'd him, but for the Conversation of this Prince and *Aboan*, and the *French* Governour he had from his Childhood, of whom I have spoken before, and who was a Man of admirable Wit, great Ingenuity and Learning; all which he had infused into his young Pupil. This *Frenchman* was banished out of his own Country, for some Heretical Notions he held: and tho he was a Man of very little Religion, he had admirable Morals, and a brave Soul.

After the total Defeat of *Jamoan's* Army, which all fled, or were left dead upon the place, they spent some time in the Camp; *Oroonoko* chusing rather to remain awhile there in his Tents, than to enter into a Palace, or live in a Court where he had so lately suffer'd so great a loss. The Officers therefore, who saw and knew his Cause of Discontent, invented all sorts of Diversions and Sports to entertain their Prince: So that what with those Amusements abroad, and others at home, that is, within their Tents, with the Persuasions, Arguments, and Care of his Friends and Servants that he more peculiarly priz'd, he wore off in time a great part of that *Chagreen*, and Torture of Despair, which the first Effects of *Imoinda's* Death had given him; insomuch as having received a thousand kind Embassies from the King, and Invitation to return to Court, he obey'd, tho with no little reluctancy: and when he did so, there was a visible change in him, and for a long time he was much more melancholy than before. But time lessens all Extremes, and reduces 'em to *Mediums*, and Unconcern: but no Motives of Beauties, tho all endeavour'd it, cou'd engage him in any sort of Amour, though he had all the Invitations to it, both from his own Youth, and others Ambitions and Designs.

Oroonoko was no sooner return'd from this last Conquest, and receiv'd at Court with all the Joy and Magnificence that cou'd be expressed to a young Victor, who was not only returned triumphant, but belov'd like a Deity, than there arriv'd in the Port an *English Ship*.

The Master of it had often before been in these Countries, and was very well known to *Oroonoko*, with whom he had traffick'd for Slaves, and had us'd to do the same with his Predecessors.

This Commander was a Man of a finer sort of Address and Conversation, better bred, and more engaging, than most of that sort of Men are; so that he seem'd rather never to have been bred out of a Court, than almost all his life at Sea. This Captain therefore was always better receiv'd at Court, than most of the Traders to those Countries were; and especially by *Oroonoko*, who was more civiliz'd, according to the *European* Mode, than any other had been, and took more delight in the *White* Nations; and, above all, Men of Parts and Wit. To this Captain he sold abundance of his Slaves; and for the Favour and Esteem he had for him, made him many Presents, and oblig'd him to stay at Court as long as possibly he cou'd. Which the Captain seem'd to take as a very great Honour done him, entertaining the Prince every day with Globes and Maps, and mathematical Discourses and Instruments; eating, drinking, hunting, and living with him with so much familiarity, that it was not to be doubted but he had gain'd very greatly upon the Heart of this gallant young Man. And the Captain, in return of all these mighty Favours, besought the Prince to honour his Vessel with his Presence, some day or other at Dinner, before he shou'd set sail: which he condescended to accept, and appointed his day. The Captain, on his part, fail'd not to have all things in a readiness, in the most magnificent order he cou'd possibly: And the day being come, the Captain, in his Boat, richly adorn'd with Carpets and Velvet-

Cushions, row'd to the shore, to receive the Prince; with another Long-Boat, where was plac'd all his Musick and Trumpets, with which *Oroonoko* was extremely delighted; who met him on the shore, attended by his *French* Governor, *Jamoan*, *Aboan*, and about an hundred of the noblest of the Youths of the Court: And after they had first carry'd the Prince on board, the Boats fetch'd the rest off; where they found a very splendid Treat, with all sorts of fine Wines; and were as well entertain'd, as 'twas possible in such a place to be.

The Prince having drunk hard of Punch, and several sorts of Wine, as did all the rest, (for great care was taken, they shou'd want nothing of that part of the Entertainment) was very merry, and in great admiration of the Ship, for he had never been in one before; so that he was curious of beholding every place where he decently might descend. The rest, no less curious, who were not quite overcome with Drinking, rambled at their pleasure *Fore* and *Aft*, as their Fancies guided 'em: So that the Captain, who had well laid his Design before, gave the Word, and seiz'd on all his Guests; they clapping great Irons suddenly on the Prince, when he was leap'd down into the Hold, to view that part of the Vessel; and locking him fast down, secur'd him. The same Treachery was us'd to all the rest; and all in one instant, in several places of the Ship, were lash'd fast in Irons, and betray'd to Slavery. That great Design over, they set all Hands to work to hoist Sail; and with as treacherous as fair a Wind they made from the Shore with this innocent and glorious Prize, who thought of nothing less than such an Entertainment.

Some have commended this Act, as brave in the Captain; but I will spare my sense of it, and leave it to my Reader to judge as he pleases. It may be easily guess'd, in what manner the Prince resented this Indignity, who may be best resembled to a Lion taken in a Toil; so he rag'd, so he struggled for Liberty, but all in vain: and they had so wisely manag'd his Fetters, that he could not use a hand in his defence to quit himself of a Life that wou'd by no means endure Slavery; nor cou'd he move from the place where he was ty'd, to any solid part of the Ship against which he might have beat his Head, and have finish'd his Disgrace that way. So that being deprived of all other means, he resolv'd to perish for want of Food; and pleas'd at last with that Thought, and toil'd and tir'd by Rage and Indignation, he laid himself down, and sullenly resolv'd upon dying, and refused all things that were brought him.

This did not a little vex the Captain, and the more so, because he found almost all of 'em of the same Humour; so that the loss of so many brave Slaves, so tall and goodly to behold, would have been very considerable: He therefore order'd one to go from him (for he wou'd not be seen himself) to *Oroonoko*, and to assure him, he was afflicted for having rashly done so unhospitable a Deed, and which could not be now remedy'd, since they were far from shore; but since he resented it in so high a nature, he assur'd him he would revoke his Resolution, and set both him and his Friends a-shore on the next Land they should touch at; and of this the Messenger gave him his Oath, provided he would resolve to live. And *Oroonoko*, whose Honour was such as he never had violated a Word in his Life himself, much less a solemn Asseveration, believ'd in an instant what this Man said; but reply'd, He expected, for a Confirmation of this, to have his shameful Fetters dismiss'd. This demand was carried to the Captain; who return'd him answer, That the Offence had been so great which he had put upon the Prince, that he durst not trust him with Liberty while he remain'd in the Ship, for fear lest by a Valour natural to him, and a Revenge that would animate that Valour, he might commit some Outrage fatal to himself, and the King his Master, to whom this Vessel did belong. To this *Oroonoko* reply'd, He would engage his Honour to behave himself in all friendly Order and Manner, and obey the command of the Captain, as he was Lord of the King's Vessel, and General of those Men under his command.

This was deliver'd to the still doubting Captain, who could not resolve to trust a Heathen, he said, upon his Parole, a Man that had no sense or notion of the God that he worshipp'd. *Oroonoko* then reply'd, He was very sorry to hear that the Captain pretended to the knowledge and worship of any Gods, who had taught him no better Principles, than not to credit as he would be credited. But they told him, the difference of their Faith occasion'd that distrust: For the Captain had protested to him upon the word of a Christian, and sworn in the name of a great God; which if he should violate, he would expect eternal Torment in the World to come. *Is that all the Obligation he has to be just to his Oath?* (reply'd *Oroonoko*) *Let him know, I swear by my Honour ; which to violate, would not only render me contemptible and despised by all brave and honest Men, and so give my self perpetual Pain, but it would be eternally offending and displeasing all Mankind ; harming, betraying, circumventing and outraging all Men. But Punishments hereafter are suffer'd by one's self ; and the World takes no Cognizance whether this GOD have reveng'd 'em, or not, 'tis done so secretly, and deferr'd so long : while the Man of no Honour suffers every moment the Scorn and Contempt of the honester World, and dies every day ignominiously in his Fame, which is more valuable than Life. I speak not this to move Belief, but to shew you how you mistake, when you imagine, That he who will violate his Honour, will keep his Word with his Gods.* So, turning from him with a disdainful Smile, he refused to answer him, when he urged him to know what Answer he should carry back to his Captain; so that he departed without saying any more.

The Captain pondering and consulting what to do, it was concluded that nothing but *Oroonoko*'s Liberty would encourage any of the rest to eat, except the *Frenchman*, whom the Captain could not pretend to keep Prisoner, but only told him, he was secured, because he might act something in favour of the Prince, but that he should be freed as soon as they came to

MRS. BEHN

Land. So that they concluded it wholly necessary to free the Prince from his Irons, that he might shew himself to the rest; that they might have an eye upon him, and that they could not fear a single Man.

This being resolv'd, to make the Obligation the greater, the Captain himself went to *Oroonoko*; where, after many Compliments, and Assurances of what he had already promis'd, he receiving from the Prince his Parole, and his Hand, for his good Behaviour, dismiss'd his Irons, and brought him to his own Cabin; where, after having treated and repos'd him a while, (for he had neither eat nor slept in four days before) he besought him to visit those obstinate People in Chains, who refus'd all manner of Sustenance; and intreated him to oblige 'em to eat, and assure 'em of that Liberty on the first Opportunity.

Oroonoko, who was too generous, not to give credit to his Words. shew'd himself to his People, who were transported with excess of Joy at the sight of their darling Prince; falling at his feet, and kissing and embracing him; believing, as some divine Oracle, all he assur'd 'em. But he besought 'em to bear their Chains with that Bravery that became those whom he had seen act so nobly in Arms; and that they could not give him greater Proofs of their Love and Friendship, since 'twas all the Security the Captain (his Friend) could have, against the Revenge, he said, they might possibly justly take, for the Injuries sustain'd by him. And they all, with one accord, assur'd him, they cou'd not suffer enough, when it was for his Repose and Safety.

After this, they no longer refus'd to eat, but took what was brought 'em, and were pleas'd with their Captivity, since by it they hoped to redeem the Prince, who, all the rest of the Voyage, was treated with all the respect due to his Birth, tho nothing could divert his Melancholy; and he wou'd often sigh for *Imoinda*, and think this a Punishment due to his Misfortune, in having left that noble Maid behind him, that fatal Night, in the *Otan*, when he fled to the Camp.

36

Possess'd with a thousand Thoughts of past Joys with this fair young Person, and a thousand Griefs for her eternal Loss, he endur'd a tedious Voyage, and at last arriv'd at the Mouth of the River of *Surinam*, a Colony belonging to the King of *England*, and where they were to deliver some part of their Slaves. There the Merchants and Gentlemen of the Country going on board, to demand those Lots of Slaves they had already agreed on; and, amongst those, the Overseers of those Plantations where I then chanc'd to be: the Captain, who had given the Word, order'd his Men to bring up those noble Slaves in Fetters, whom I have spoken of; and having put 'em, some in one, and some in other Lots, with Women and Children (which they call *Pickaninies*) they sold 'em off, as Slaves, to several Merchants and Gentlemen; not putting any two in one Lot, because they would separate 'em far from each other; nor daring to trust 'em together, lest Rage and Courage should put 'em upon contriving some great Action, to the ruin of the Colony.

Oroonoko was first seiz'd on, and sold to our Overseer, who had the first Lot, with seventeen more of all sorts and sizes, but not one of Quality with him. When he saw this, he found what they meant; for, as I said, he understood *English* pretty well; and being wholly unarm'd and defenceless, so as it was in vain to make any Resistance, he only beheld the Captain with a Look all fierce and disdainful, upbraiding him with Eyes that forc'd Blushes on his guilty Cheeks, he only cry'd in passing over the side of the Ship; *Farewel, Sir, 'tis worth my Sufferings, to gain so true a Knowledge both of you, and of your Gods by whom you swear.* And desiring those that held him to forbear their Pains, and telling 'em he would make no Resistance, he cry'd, *Come, my Fellow-Slaves, let us descend, and see if we can meet with more Honour and Honesty in the next World we shall touch upon.* So he nimbly leapt into the Boat, and shewing no more concern, suffer'd himself to be row'd up the River, with his seventeen Companions.

The Gentleman that bought him, was a young *Cornish* Gentleman, whose Name was *Trefry*; a Man of great Wit, and fine Learning, and was carry'd into those Parts by the Lord-Governour, to manage all his Affairs. He reflecting on the last Words of *Oroonoko* to the Captain, and beholding the Richness of his Vest, no sooner came into the Boat, but he fix'd his Eyes on him; and finding something so extraordinary in his Face, his Shape and Mein, a greatness of Look, and haughtiness in his Air, and finding he spoke *English*, had a great mind to be enquiring into his Quality and Fortune: which, though *Oroonoko* endeavour'd to hide, by only confessing he was above the Rank of common Slaves; *Trefry* soon found he was yet something greater than he confess'd; and from that moment began to conceive so vast an Esteem for him, that he ever after lov'd him as his dearest Brother, and shew'd him all the Civilities due to so great a Man.

Trefry was a very good Mathematician, and a Linguist; could speak *French* and *Spanish*; and in the three days they remain'd in the Boat (for so long were they going from the Ship to the Plantation) he entertain'd *Oroonoko* so agreeably with his Art and Discourse, that he was no less pleas'd with *Trefry*, than he was with the Prince; and he thought himself, at least, fortunate in this, that since he was a Slave, as long as he would suffer himself to remain so, he had a Man of so excellent Wit and Parts for a Master. So that before they had finish'd their Voyage up the River, he made no scruple of declaring to *Trefry* all his Fortunes, and most part of what I have here related, and put himself wholly into the hands of his new Friend, whom he found resenting all the Injuries were done him, and was charm'd with all the Greatnesses of his Actions; which were recited with that Modesty, and delicate Sense, as wholly vanquished him, and subdu'd him to his Interest. And he promised him on his Word and Honour he wou'd find the Means to re-conduct him to his own Country again; assuring him, he had a perfect Abhorrence of so dishonourable an Action; and that he would sooner have dy'd, than have been the Author of such a Perfidy. He found the Prince was very much concerned to know what became of his Friends, and how they took their Slavery; and *Trefry* promised to take care about the enquiring after their Condition, and that he should have an account of 'em.

Though, as *Oroonoko* afterwards said, he had little reason to credit the Words of a *Backearary*; yet he knew not why, but he saw a kind of Sincerity, and awful Truth in the Face of *Trefry*; he saw an Honesty in his Eyes, and he found him wise and witty enough to understand Honour: for it was one of his Maxims, *A Man of Wit cou'd not be a Knave or Villain.*

In their Passage up the River, they put in at several Houses for Refreshment; and ever when they landed, numbers of People would flock to behold this Man: not but their Eyes were daily entertain'd with the sight of Slaves, but the Fame of *Oroonoko* was gone before him, and all People were in admiration of his Beauty. Besides, he had a rich Habit on, in which he was taken, so different from the rest, and which the Captain cou'd not strip him of, because he was forc'd to surprize his Person in the minute he sold him. When he found his Habit made him liable, as he thought, to be gazed at the more, he begged *Trefry* to give him something more befitting a Slave, which he did, and took off his Robes: Nevertheless he shone thro all, and his *Osenbrigs* (a sort of brown *Holland* Suit he had on) cou'd not conceal the Graces of his Looks and Mein; and he had no less Admirers than when he had his dazling Habit on: The Royal Youth appear'd in spight of the Slave, and People cou'd not help treating him after a different manner, without designing it. As soon as they approached him, they venerated and esteemed him; his Eyes insensibly commanded Respect, and his Behaviour insinuated it into every Soul. So that there was nothing talked of but this young and gallant Slave, even by those who yet knew not that he was a Prince.

MRS. BEHN

I ought to tell you, that the Christians never buy any Slaves but they give 'em some Name of their own, their native ones being likely very barbarous, and hard to pronounce; so that Mr. *Trefry* gave *Oroonoko* that of *Cæsar*; which Name will live in that Country as long as that (scarce more) glorious one of the great *Roman*: for 'tis most evident he wanted no part of the personal Courage of that *Cæsar*, and acted things as memorable, had they been done in some part of the World replenished with People and Historians, that might have given him his due. But his Misfortune was, to fall in an obscure World, that afforded only a Female Pen to celebrate his Fame; though I doubt not but it had lived from others Endeavours, if the *Dutch*, who immediately after his time took that Country, had not killed, banished and dispersed all those that were capable of giving the World this great Man's Life, much better than I have done. And Mr. *Trefry*, who designed it, dy'd before he began it, and bemoan'd himself for not having undertook it in time.

For the future therefore I must call *Oroonoko Cæsar*; since by that Name only he was known in our Western World, and by that Name he was received on shore at *Parham-House*, where he was destin'd a Slave. But if the King himself (God bless him) had come ashore, there cou'd not have been greater Expectation by all the whole Plantation, and those neighbouring ones, than was on ours at that time; and he was received more like a Governour than a Slave: notwithstanding, as the Custom was, they assigned him his Portion of Land, his House and his Business up in the Plantation. But as it was more for Form, than any Design to put him to his Task, he endured no more of the Slave but the Name, and remain'd some days in the House, receiving all Visits that were made him, without stirring towards that part of the Plantation where the *Negroes* were.

At last, he wou'd needs go view his Land, his House, and the Business assign'd him. But he no sooner came

40

to the Houses of the Slaves, which are like a little Town by it self, the *Negroes* all having left work, but they all came forth to behold him, and found he was that Prince who had, at several times, sold most of 'em to these Parts; and from a Veneration they pay to great Men, especially if they know 'em, and from the Surprize and Awe they had at the sight of him, they all cast themselves at his feet, crying out, in their Language, *Live, O King! Long live, O King!* and kissing his Feet, paid him even Divine Homage.

Several *English* Gentlemen were with him, and what Mr. *Trefry* had told 'em was here confirm'd; of which he himself before had no other Witness than *Cæsar* himself: But he was infinitely glad to find his Grandeur confirmed by the Adoration of all the Slaves.

Cæsar troubled with their Over-Joy, and Over-Ceremony, besought 'em to rise, and to receive him as their Fellow-Slave; assuring them he was no better. At which they set up with one accord a most terrible and hideous mourning and condoling, which he and the *English* had much ado to appease: but at last they prevailed with 'em, and they prepared all their barbarous Musick, and every one kill'd and dress'd something of his own Stock (for every Family has their Land apart, on which, at their leisure-times, they breed all eatable things) and clubbing it together, made a most magnificent Supper, inviting their *Grandee Captain*, their *Prince*, to honour it with his Presence; which he did, and several *English* with him, where they all waited on him, some playing, others dancing before him all the time, according to the Manners of their several Nations, and with unweary'd Industry endeavouring to please and delight him.

While they sat at Meat, Mr. *Trefry* told *Cæsar*, that most of these young Slaves were undone in love with a fine She-Slave, whom they had had about six Months on their Land; the Prince, who never heard the Name of *Love* without a Sigh, nor any mention of it without the Curiosity of examining further into that Tale, which of all Discourses was most agreeable to him, asked, how they came to be so unhappy, as to be all undone for one fair Slave? *Trefry*, who was naturally amorous, and lov'd to talk of Love as well as any body, proceeded to tell him, they had the most charming Black that ever was beheld on their Plantation, about fifteen or sixteen Years old, as he guess'd; that for his part he had done nothing but sigh for her ever since she came; and that all the White Beauties he had seen, never charm'd him so absolutely as this fine Creature had done; and that no Man, of any Nation, ever beheld her that did not fall in love with her; and that she had all the Slaves perpetually at her feet; and the whole Country resounded with the Fame of *Clemene*, for so (said he) we have christen'd her: but she denies us all with such a noble Disdain, that 'tis a Miracle to see, that she who can give such eternal Desires, should her self be all Ice and all Unconcern. She is adorn'd with the most graceful Modesty that ever beautify'd Youth; the softest Sigher—that, if she were capable of Love, one would swear she languished for some absent happy Man; and so retired, as if she fear'd a Rape even from the God of Day, or that the Breezes wou'd steal Kisses from her delicate Mouth. Her Task of Work, some sighing Lover every day makes it his petition to perform for her; which she accepts blushing, and with reluctancy, for fear he will ask her a Look for a Recompence, which he dares not presume to hope; so great an Awe she strikes into the Hearts of her Admirers. *I do not wonder* (reply'd the Prince) *that Clemene should refuse Slaves, being, as you say, so beautiful; but wonder how she escapes those that can entertain her as you can do: or why, being your Slave, you do not oblige her to yield? I confess* (said *Trefry*) *when I have, against her will, entertained her with Love so long, as to be transported with my Passion even above Decency, I have been ready to make use of those Advantages of Strength and Force Nature has given me: But Oh! she disarms me with that Modesty and Weeping, so tender and so moving, that*

42

I retire, and thank my Stars she overcame me. The
Company laugh'd at his Civility to a Slave, and *Cæsar*
only applauded the Nobleness of his Passion and Nature,
since that Slave might be noble, or, what was better,
have true Notions of Honour and Vertue in her. Thus
passed they this Night, after having received from the
Slaves all imaginable Respect and Obedience.

The next day, *Trefry* ask'd *Cæsar* to walk when the Heat
was allay'd, and designedly carry'd him by the Cottage
of the fair Slave; and told him she whom he spoke of
last night lived there retir'd: *But* (says he) *I would not
wish you to approach ; for I am sure you will be in love
as soon as you behold her.* *Cæsar* assured him, he was
proof against all the Charms of that Sex; and that if
he imagined his Heart could be so perfidious to love
again, after *Imoinda*, he believed he should tear it from
his Bosom. They had no sooner spoke, but a little
Shock-Dog, that *Clemene* had presented her, which she
took great delight in, ran out; and she, not knowing
any body was there, ran to get it in again, and bolted
out on those who were just speaking of her: when
seeing them, she would have run in again. but *Trefry*
caught her by the Hand, and cry'd, Clemene, *however
you fly a Lover, you ought to pay some respect to this
Stranger*, (pointing to *Cæsar*.) But she, as if she had
resolved never to raise her Eyes to the Face of a Man
again, bent 'em the more to the Earth, when he spoke,
and gave the Prince the leisure to look the more at her.
There needed no long gazing, or Consideration, to ex-
amine who this fair Creature was; he soon saw *Imoinda*
all over her; in a minute he saw her Face, her Shape, her
Air, her Modesty, and all that call'd forth his Soul with
Joy at his Eyes, and left his Body destitute of almost
Life: it stood without Motion, and for a Minute knew
not that it had a Being; and, I believe, he had never
come to himself, so oppress'd he was with Over-joy, if
he had not met with this allay, that he perceived
Imoinda fall dead in the hands of *Trefry*. This awaken'd
him, and he ran to her aid, and caught her in his Arms,

where by degrees she came to her self; and 'tis needless to tell with what Transports, what Exstasies of Joy, they both awhile beheld each other, without speaking; then snatched each other to their Arms; then gaze again, as if they still doubted whether they possess'd the Blessing they grasped: but when they recover'd their Speech, 'tis not to be imagined what tender things they express'd to each other; wondring what strange Fate had brought them again together. They soon inform'd each other of their Fortunes, and equally bewail'd their Fate; but at the same time they mutually protested, that even Fetters and Slavery were soft and easy, and would be supported with Joy and Pleasure, while they cou'd be so happy to possess each other, and to be able to make good their Vows. *Cæsar* swore he disdained the Empire of the World, while he could behold his *Imoinda*; and she despised Grandeur and Pomp, those Vanities of her Sex, when she could gaze on *Oroonoko*. He ador'd the very Cottage where she resided, and said, That little Inch of the World would give him more Happiness than all the Universe cou'd do; and she vow'd, it was a Palace, while adorned with the Presence of *Oroonoko*.

Trefry was infinitely pleased with this Novel, and found this *Clemene* was the fair Mistress of whom *Cæsar* had before spoke; and was not a little satisfy'd, that Heaven was so kind to the Prince as to sweeten his Misfortunes by so lucky an Accident; and leaving the Lovers to themselves, was impatient to come down to *Parham-House* (which was on the same Plantation) to give me an account of what had hapned. I was as impatient to make these Lovers a Visit, having already made a Friendship with *Cæsar*, and from his own Mouth learned what I have related; which was confirmed by his *Frenchman*, who was set on shore to seek his Fortune, and of whom they cou'd not make a Slave, because a Christian; and he came daily to *Parham-Hill* to see and pay his Respects to his Pupil Prince. So that concerning and interesting my self in all that related to

44

Cæsar, whom I had assured of Liberty as soon as the Governour arrived, I hasted presently to the Place where these Lovers were, and was infinitely glad to find this beautiful young Slave (who had already gain'd all our Esteems, for her Modesty and her extraordinary Prettiness) to be the same I had heard *Cæsar* speak so much of. One may imagine then we paid her a treble Respect; and tho from her being carved in fine Flowers and Birds all over her Body, we took her to be of Quality before, yet when we knew *Clemene* was *Imoinda*, we could not enough admire her.

I had forgot to tell you, that those who are nobly born of that Country, are so delicately cut and raised all over the Fore-part of the Trunk of their Bodies, that it looks as if it were japan'd, the Works being raised like high Point round the edges of the Flowers. Some are only carved with a little Flower, or Bird, at the sides of the Temples, as was *Cæsar*; and those who are so carved over the Body, resemble our antient *Picts* that are figur'd in the Chronicles, but these Carvings are more delicate.

From that happy day *Cæsar* took *Clemene* for his Wife, to the general joy of all People; and there was as much Magnificence as the Country would afford at the Celebration of this Wedding: and in a very short time after she conceived with Child, which made *Cæsar* even adore her, knowing he was the last of his great Race. This new Accident made him more impatient of Liberty, and he was every day treating with *Trefry* for his and *Clemene's* Liberty, and offer'd either Gold, or a vast quantity of Slaves, which should be paid before they let him go, provided he could have any Security that he should go when his Ransom was paid. They fed him from day to day with Promises, and delay'd him till the Lord-Governour should come; so that he began to suspect them of Falshood, and that they would delay him till the time of his Wife's Delivery, and make a Slave of that too: for all the Breed is theirs to whom the Parents belong. This Thought made him very uneasy, and his Sullenness gave them some Jealousies of him; so that I was obliged, by some Persons who fear'd a Mutiny (which is very fatal sometimes in those Colonies that abound so with Slaves, that they exceed the Whites in vast numbers) to discourse with *Cæsar*, and to give him all the Satisfaction I possibly could: They knew he and *Clemene* were scarce an Hour in a Day from my Lodgings; that they eat with me, and that I oblig'd 'em in all things I was capable of. I entertained them with the Loves of the *Romans*, and great Men, which charmed him to my Company; and her, with teaching her all the pretty Works that I was Mistress of, and telling her Stories of Nuns, and endeavouring to bring her to the Knowledg of the true God: But of all Discourses, *Cæsar* liked that the worst, and would never be reconciled to our Notions of the Trinity, of which he ever made a Jest; it was a Riddle he said would turn his Brain to conceive, and one cou'd not make him understand what Faith was. However, these Conversations fail'd not altogether so well to divert him, that he liked the Company of us Women much above the Men, for he could not drink, and he is but an ill Companion in that Country that cannot. So that obliging him to love us very well, we had all the Liberty of Speech with him, especially my self, whom he call'd his *Great Mistress*; and indeed my Word would go a great way with him. For these Reasons I had opportunity to take notice to him, that he was not well pleased of late, as he used to be; was more retired and thoughtful; and told him, I took it ill he shou'd suspect we wou'd break our Words with him, and not permit both him and *Clemene* to return to his own Kingdom, which was not so long a way, but when he was once on his Voyage he wou'd quickly arrive there. He made me some Answers that shew'd a doubt in him, which made me ask, what advantage it would be to doubt? It would but give us a fear of him, and possibly compel us to treat him so as I should be very loth to behold: that is, it might occasion his Confinement. Perhaps this was not so luckily spoke of me, for I perceiv'd he resented that Word, which I strove to soften again in vain: However, he assur'd me, that whatsoever Resolutions he should take, he would act nothing upon the *White* People; and as for my self, and those upon that *Plantation* where he was, he would sooner forfeit his eternal Liberty, and Life it self, than lift his Hand against his greatest Enemy on that place. He besought me to suffer no Fears upon his account, for he could do nothing that Honour should not dictate; but he accus'd himself for having suffer'd Slavery so long: yet he charg'd that weakness on Love alone, who was capable of making him neglect even Glory it self; and, for which, now he reproaches himself every moment of the Day. Much more to this effect he spoke, with an Air impatient enough to make me know he would not be long in Bondage; and though he suffer'd only the Name of a Slave, and had nothing of the Toil and Labour of one, yet that was sufficient to render him uneasy; and he had been too long idle, who us'd to be always in Action, and in Arms. He had a Spirit all rough and fierce, and that could not be tam'd to lazy Rest; and though all Endeavours were us'd to exercise himself in such Actions and Sports as this World afforded, as Running, Wrestling, Pitching the Bar, Hunting and Fishing, Chasing and Killing *Tygers* of a monstrous size, which this Continent affords in abundance; and wonderful *Snakes*, such as *Alexander* is reported to have encounter'd at the River of *Amazons*, and which *Cæsar* took great delight to overcome; yet these were not Actions great enough for his large Soul, which was still panting after more renown'd Actions.

Before I parted that day with him, I got, with much-ado, a Promise from him to rest yet a little longer with patience, and wait the coming of the Lord Governour, who was every day expected on our shore: he assur'd me he would, and this Promise he desired me to know was given perfectly in complaisance to me, in whom he had an intire Confidence.

After this, I neither thought it convenient to trust him much out of our view, nor did the Country, who fear'd him; but with one accord it was advis'd to treat him fairly, and oblige him to remain within such a compass, and that he should be permitted, as seldom as could be, to go up to the Plantations of the *Negroes*; or, if he did, to be accompany'd by some that should be rather in appearance Attendants than Spies. This Care was for some time taken, and *Cæsar* look'd upon it as a Mark of extraordinary Respect, and was glad his discontent had oblig'd 'em to be more observant to him; he received new assurance from the Overseer, which was confirmed to him by the Opinion of all the Gentlemen of the Country, who made their court to him. During this time that we had his Company more frequently than hitherto we had had, it may not be unpleasant to relate to you the Diversions we entertain'd him with, or rather he us.

My stay was to be short in that Country; because my Father dy'd at Sea. and never arriv'd to possess the Honour design'd him, (which was Lieutenant-General of six and thirty Islands, besides the Continent of *Surinam*) nor the Advantages he hop'd to reap by them: so that though we were oblig'd to continue on our Voyage, we did not intend to stay upon the Place. Though, in a word, I must say thus much of it; that certainly had his late Majesty, of sacred Memory, but seen and known what a vast and charming World he had been Master of in that Continent, he would never have parted so easily with it to the *Dutch*. 'Tis a Continent whose vast Extent was never yet known, and may contain more noble Earth than all the Universe beside; for, they say, it reaches from East to West one way as far as *China*, and another to *Peru*: It affords all things both for Beauty and Use; 'tis there eternal Spring, always the very Months of *April, May*, and *June*; the Shades are perpetual, the Trees bearing at once all degrees of Leaves and Fruit, from blooming Buds to ripe Autumn: Groves of Oranges, Lemons,

Citrons, Figs, Nutmegs, and noble Aromaticks, continually bearing their Fragrancies. The Trees appearing all like Nosegays adorn'd with Flowers of different kinds, some are all White, some Purple, some Scarlet, some Blue, some Yellow; bearing at the same time ripe Fruit, and blooming Young, or producing every day new. The very Wood of all these Trees has an intrinsick Value above common Timber; for they are, when cut, of different Colours, glorious to behold, and bear a price considerable, to inlay withal. Besides this, they yield rich Balm, and Gums; so that we make our Candles of such an aromatick Substance, as does not only give a sufficient Light, but, as they burn, they cast their Perfumes all about. Cedar is the common firing, and all the Houses are built with it. The very Meat we eat, when set on the Table, if it be native, I mean of the Country, perfumes the whole Room; especially a little Beast call'd an *Armadilly*, a thing which I can liken to nothing so well as a *Rhinoceros*; 'tis all in white Armour, so jointed, that it moves as well in it, as if it had nothing on: this Beast is about the bigness of a Pig of six Weeks old. But it were endless to give an account of all the divers wonderful and strange Things that Country affords, and which we took a very great delight to go in search of; tho those Adventures are oftentimes fatal, and at least dangerous: But while we had *Cæsar* in our company on these Designs, we fear'd no harm, nor suffer'd any.

As soon as I came into the Country, the best House in it was presented me, call'd *St. John's Hill*: It stood on a vast Rock of white Marble, at the foot of which the River ran a vast depth down, and not to be descended on that side; the little Waves still dashing and washing the foot of this Rock, made the softest Murmurs and Purlings in the World; and the opposite Bank was adorn'd with such vast quantities of different Flowers eternally blowing, and every Day and Hour new, fenc'd behind 'em with lofty Trees of a thousand rare Forms and Colours, that the Prospect was the most ravishing that Sands can create. On the edge of this white Rock, towards the River, was a Walk or Grove of Orange and Lemon-Trees, about half the length of the *Mall* here, flowery and fruit-bearing Branches met at the top, and hinder'd the Sun, whose Rays are very fierce there, from entering a Beam into the Grove; and the cool Air that came from the River, made it not only fit to entertain People in, at all the hottest hours of the day, but refresh'd the sweet Blossoms, and made it always sweet and charming; and sure, the whole Globe of the World cannot shew so delightful a Place as this Grove was: Not all the Gardens of boasted *Italy* can produce a Shade to out-vie this, which Nature had join'd with Art to render so exceeding fine; and 'tis a marvel to see how such vast Trees, as big as *English* Oaks, could take footing on so solid a Rock, and in so little Earth as cover'd that Rock: But all things by Nature there are rare, delightful and wonderful. But to our Sports.

Sometimes we would go surprizing, and in search of young *Tygers* in their Dens, watching when the old ones went forth to forage for Prey; and oftentimes we have been in great danger, and have fled apace for our Lives, when surpriz'd by the Dams. But once, above all other times, we went on this Design, and *Cæsar* was with us; who had no sooner stoln a young *Tyger* from her Nest, but going off, we encounter'd the Dam, bearing a Buttock of a Cow, which she had torn off with her mighty Paw, and going with it towards her Den: we had only four Women, *Cæsar*, and an *English* Gentleman, Brother to *Harry Martin* the great *Oliverian*; we found there was no escaping this enraged and ravenous Beast. However, we Women fled as fast as we could from it; but our Heels had not saved our Lives, if *Cæsar* had not laid down his *Cub*, when he found the *Tyger* quit her Prey to make the more speed towards him; and taking Mr. *Martin's* Sword, desired him to stand aside, or follow the Ladies. He obey'd him; and *Cæsar* met this monstrous Beast of mighty Size, and vast Limbs, who came with open Jaws upon him; and fixing his awful

stern Eyes full upon those of the Beast, and putting
himself into a very steddy and good aiming Posture of
Defence, ran his Sword quite through her Breast down
to her very Heart, home to the Hilt of the Sword: the
dying Beast stretch'd forth her Paw, and going to grasp
his Thigh, surpriz'd with death in that very moment,
did him no other harm than fixing her long Nails in his
Flesh very deep, feebly wounded him, but could not grasp
the Flesh to tear off any. When he had done this, he
hollow'd to us to return: which, after some assurance
of his Victory, we did, and found him lugging out the
Sword from the Bosom of the *Tyger*, who was laid in
her Blood on the ground; he took up the *Cub*, and with
an unconcern that had nothing of the Joy or Gladness
of a Victory, he came and laid the Whelp at my feet.
We all extremely wonder'd at his daring, and at the
bigness of the Beast, which was about the height of an
Heifer, but of mighty great and strong Limbs.

Another time being in the Woods, he kill'd a *Tyger*
which had long infested that Part, and borne away
abundance of Sheep and Oxen, and other things that
were for the support of those to whom they belong'd:
abundance of People assail'd this Beast, some affirming
they had shot her with several Bullets quite through
the Body, at several times; and some swearing they
shot her through the very Heart, and they believ'd she
was a Devil, rather than a mortal thing. *Cæsar* had
often said, he had a mind to encounter this Monster,
and spoke with several Gentlemen who had attempted
her; one crying, I shot her with so many poison'd
Arrows, another with his Gun in this part of her, and
another in that: so that he remarking all these places
where she was shot, fancy'd still he should overcome
her, by giving her another sort of a Wound than any
had yet done, and one day said (at the Table) *What
Trophies and Garlands, Ladies, will you make me, if I
bring you home the Heart of this ravenous Beast, that eats
up all your Lambs and Pigs ?* We all promis'd he should
be rewarded at all our hands. So taking a Bow, which

he chose out of a great many, he went up into the Wood, with two Gentlemen, where he imagin'd this Devourer to be; they had not past very far in it, but they heard her Voice, growling and grumbling, as if she were pleas'd with something she was doing. When they came in view, they found her muzzling in the Belly of a new ravish'd Sheep, which she had torn open; and seeing her self approach'd, she took fast hold of her Prey with her fore Paws, and set a very fierce raging Look on *Cæsar*, without offering to approach him, for fear at the same time of losing what she had in possession. So that *Cæsar* remain'd a good while, only taking aim, and getting an opportunity to shoot her where he design'd: 'twas some time before he could accomplish it; and to wound her, and not kill her, would but have enrag'd her the more, and endanger'd him. He had a Quiver of Arrows at his side, so that if one fail'd, he could be supply'd; at last, retiring a little, he gave her opportunity to eat, for he found she was ravenous, and fell to as soon as she saw him retire, being more eager of her Prey, than of doing new Mischiefs: when he going softly to one side of her, and hiding his Person behind certain Herbage that grew high and thick, he took so good aim, that, as he intended, he shot her just into the Eye, and the Arrow was sent with so good a will, and so sure a hand, that it stuck in her Brain, and made her caper, and become mad for a moment or two; but being seconded by another Arrow, she fell dead upon the Prey. *Cæsar* cut her open with a Knife, to see where those Wounds were that had been reported to him, and why she did not die of 'em. But I shall now relate a thing that, possibly, will find no credit among Men; because 'tis a Notion commonly receiv'd with us, That nothing can receive a Wound in the Heart and live: But when the Heart of this courageous Animal was taken out, there were seven Bullets of Lead in it, the Wound seam'd up with great Scars, and she liv'd with the Bullets a great while, for it was long since they were shot: This Heart

the Conqueror brought up to us, and 'twas a very great
Curiosity, which all the Country came to see; and
which gave *Cæsar* occasion of many fine Discourses, of
Accidents in War, and strange Escapes.

At other times he would go a Fishing; and discoursing
on that Diversion, he found we had in that Country a
very strange Fish, call'd a *Numb-Eel* (an *Eel* of which
I have eaten) that while it is alive, it has a Quality so
cold, that those who are Angling, though with a Line
of ever so great a length, with a Rod at the end of it,
it shall, in the same minute the Bait is touch'd by this
Eel, seize him or her that holds the Rod with a numbness, that shall deprive 'em of Sense for a while; and
some have fallen into the Water, and others drop'd, as
dead, on the Banks of the Rivers where they stood, as
soon as this Fish touches the Bait. *Cæsar* us'd to laugh
at this, and believ'd it impossible a Man could lose his
Force at the touch of a Fish; and could not understand
that Philosophy, that a cold Quality should be of that
nature; however, he had a great Curiosity to try whether
it would have the same effect on him it had on others,
and often try'd, but in vain. At last, the sought-for
Fish came to the Bait, as he stood angling on the Bank;
and instead of throwing away the Rod, or giving it a
sudden twitch out of the Water, whereby he might
have caught both the *Eel*, and have dismiss'd the Rod,
before it could have too much power over him; for
Experiment-sake, he grasp'd it but the harder, and
fainting fell into the River; and being still possess'd
of the Rod, the Tide carry'd him, senseless as he was, a
great way, till an *Indian* Boat took him up; and perceiv'd, when they touch'd him, a Numbness seize them,
and by that knew the Rod was in his hand; which
with a Paddle, (that is, a short Oar) they struck away,
and snatcht it into the Boat, *Eel* and all. If *Cæsar*
was almost dead, with the effect of this Fish, he was
more so with that of the Water, where he had remain'd
the space of going a League, and they found they had
much ado to bring him back to Life; but at last they

did, and brought him home, where he was in a few hours well recover'd and refresh'd, and not a little asham'd to find he should be overcome by an *Eel*, and that all the People, who heard his Defiance, would laugh at him. But we chear'd him up; and he being convinc'd, we had the *Eel* at Supper, which was a quarter of an Ell about, and most delicate Meat; and was of the more value, since it cost so dear as almost the Life of so gallant a Man.

About this time we were in many mortal Fears, about some Disputes the *English* had with the *Indians*; so that we could scarce trust our selves, without great Numbers, to go to any *Indian* Towns or Place where they abode, for fear they should fall upon us, as they did immediately after my coming away; and the Place being in the Possession of the *Dutch*, they us'd them not so civilly as the *English*: so that they cut in pieces all they could take, getting into Houses, and hanging up the Mother, and all her Children about her; and cut a Footman, I left behind me, all in Joints, and nail'd him to Trees.

This Feud began while I was there; so that I lost half the Satisfaction I propos'd, in not seeing and visiting the *Indian* Towns. But one day, bemoaning of our Misfortunes upon this account, *Cæsar* told us, we need not fear, for if we had a mind to go, he would undertake to be our Guard. Some would, but most would not venture: About Eighteen of us resolv'd, and took Barge; and after eight days, arriv'd near an *Indian* Town: But approaching it, the Hearts of some of our Company fail'd, and they would not venture on Shore; so we poll'd, who would, and who would not. For my part, I said, if *Cæsar* would, I would go. He resolv'd; so did my Brother, and my Woman, a Maid of good Courage. Now, none of us speaking the Language of the People, and imagining we should have a half Diversion in gazing only; and not knowing what they said, we took a Fisherman that liv'd at the Mouth of the River, who had been a long Inhabitant there, and oblig'd him to go with us: But because he was known to the *Indians*, as trading among 'em, and being, by long living there, become a perfect *Indian* in colour, we, who had a mind to surprize 'em, by making them see something they never had seen, (that is, *White* People) resolv'd only my self, my Brother and Woman should go: so *Cæsar*, the Fisherman, and the rest, hiding behind some thick Reeds and Flowers that grew in the Banks, let us pass on towards the Town, which was on the Bank of the River all along. A little distant from the Houses, or Huts, we saw some dancing, others busy'd in fetching and carrying of Water from the River. They had no sooner spy'd us, but they set up a loud Cry, that frighted us at first; we thought it had been for those that should kill us, but it seems it was of Wonder and Amazement. They were all naked; and we were dress'd, so as is most commode for the hot Countries, very glittering and rich; so that we appear'd extremely fine: my own Hair was cut short, and I had a taffety Cap, with black Feathers on my Head; my Brother was in a Stuff-Suit, with silver Loops and Buttons, and abundance of green Ribbon. This was all infinitely surprizing to them; and because we saw them stand still till we approach'd 'em, we took heart and advanc'd, came up to 'em, and offer'd 'em our Hands; which they took, and look'd on us round about, calling still for more Company; who came swarming out, all wondering, and crying out *Tepeeme*: taking their Hair up in their Hands, and spreading it wide to those they call'd out to; as if they would say (as indeed it signify'd) *Numberless Wonders*, or not to be recounted, no more than to number the Hair of their Heads. By degrees they grew more bold, and from gazing upon us round, they touch'd us, laying their Hands upon all the Features of our Faces, feeling our Breasts and Arms, taking up one Petticoat, then wondering to see another; admiring our Shoes and Stockings, but more our Garters, which we gave 'em, and they ty'd about their Legs, being lac'd with silver Lace at the ends;

for they much esteem any shining things. In fine, we suffer'd 'em to survey us as they pleas'd, and we thought they would never have done admiring us. When *Cæsar*, and the rest, saw we were receiv'd with such wonder, they came up to us; and finding the *Indian* Trader whom they knew, (for 'tis by these Fishermen, call'd *Indian* Traders, we hold a Commerce with 'em; for they love not to go far from home, and we never go to them) when they saw him therefore, they set up a new Joy, and cry'd in their Language, *Oh! here's our* Tiguamy, *and we shall now know whether those things can speak.* So advancing to him, some of 'em gave him their Hands, and cry'd, *Amora Tiguamy*; which is as much as, *How do you do*; or, *welcome Friend*: and all, with one din, began to gabble to him, and ask'd, if we had Sense and Wit? If we could talk of Affairs of Life and War, as they could do? If we could hunt, swim, and do a thousand things they use? He answer'd 'em, We could. Then they invited us into their Houses, and dress'd Venison and Buffalo for us; and, going out, gather'd a Leaf of a Tree, called a *Sarumbo* Leaf, of six Yards long, and spread it on the Ground for a Table-cloth; and cutting another in pieces, instead of Plates, set us on little low *Indian*-Stools, which they cut out of one entire piece of Wood, and paint in a sort of Japan-work. They serve every one their Mess on these pieces of Leaves; and it was very good, but too high-season'd with Pepper. When we had eat, my Brother and I took out our Flutes, and play'd to 'em, which gave 'em new wonder; and I soon perceiv'd, by an admiration that is natural to these People, and by the extreme Ignorance and Simplicity of 'em, it were not difficult to establish any unknown or extravagant Religion among them, and to impose any Notions or Fictions upon 'em. For seeing a Kinsman of mine set some Paper on fire with a Burning-glass, a Trick they had never before seen, they were like to have ador'd him for a God, and begg'd he would give 'em the Characters or Figures of his Name, that they might oppose it against

Winds and Storms: which he did, and they held it up in those Seasons, and fancy'd it had a Charm to conquer them, and kept it like a holy Relique. They are very superstitious, and call'd him the great *Peeie*, that is, *Prophet*. They shewed us their *Indian Peeie*, a Youth of about sixteen Years old, as handsom as Nature could make a Man. They consecrate a beautiful Youth from his Infancy, and all Arts are used to compleat him in the finest manner, both in Beauty and Shape: He is bred to all the little arts and cunning they are capable of; to all the legerdemain Tricks, and sleight of Hand, whereby he imposes upon the Rabble; and is both a Doctor in Physick and Divinity: And by these Tricks makes the sick believe he sometimes eases their Pains, by drawing from the afflicted Part little Serpents, or odd Flies, or Worms, or any strange thing; and though they have besides undoubted good Remedies for almost all their Diseases, they cure the Patient more by Fancy than by Medicines, and make themselves feared, loved, and reverenced. This young *Peeie* had a very young Wife, who seeing my Brother kiss her, came running and kiss'd me. After this they kiss'd one another, and made it a very great Jest, it being so novel; and rew Admiration and Laughing went round the Multitude, that they never will forget that Ceremony, never before us'd or known. *Cæsar* had a mind to see and talk with their War-Captains, and we were conducted to one of their Houses; where we beheld several of the great Captains, who had been at Council: But so frightful a Vision it was to see 'em, no Fancy can create; no sad Dreams can represent so dreadful a Spectacle. For my part, I took 'em for Hobgoblins, or Fiends, rather than Men: but however their Shapes appear'd, their Souls were very humane and noble; but some wanted their Noses, some their Lips, some both Noses and Lips, some their Ears, and others cut through each Cheek, with long Slashes, through which their Teeth appear'd: they had several other formidable Wounds and Scars, or rather Dismembrings. They had *Comitia's*, or little

Aprons before 'em; and Girdles of Cotton, with their Knives naked stuck in it; a Bow at their Back, and a Quiver of Arrows on their Thighs; and most had Feathers on their Heads of divers Colours. They cry'd *Amora Tiguame* to us, at our entrance, and were pleas'd we said as much to them: They seated us, and gave us Drink of the best sort, and wonder'd as much as the others had done before, to see us. *Cæsar* was marvelling as much at their Faces, wondring how they should all be so wounded in War; he was impatient to know how they all came by those frightful Marks of Rage or Malice, rather than Wounds got in noble Battel: They told us by our Interpreter, That when any War was waging, two Men, chosen out by some old Captain whose fighting was past, and who could only teach the Theory of War, were to stand in competition for the Generalship, or great War-Captain; and being brought before the old Judges, now past Labour, they are ask'd, What they dare do, to shew they are worthy to lead an Army? When he who is first ask'd, making no reply, cuts off his Nose, and throws it contemptibly on the ground; and the other does something to himself that he thinks surpasses him, and perhaps deprives himself of Lips and an Eye: so they slash on till one gives out, and many have dy'd in this Debate. And it's by a passive Valour they shew and prove their Activity; a sort of Courage too brutal to be applauded by our *Black* Hero; nevertheless, he express'd his Esteem of 'em.

In this Voyage *Cæsar* begat so good an understanding between the *Indians* and the *English*, that there were no more Fears or Heart-burnings during our stay, but we had a perfect, open, and free Trade with 'em. Many things remarkable, and worthy reciting, we met with in this short Voyage; because *Cæsar* made it his business to search out and provide for our Entertainment, especially to please his dearly ador'd *Imoinda*, who was a sharer in all our Adventures; we being resolv'd to make her Chains as easy as we could, and to compliment the Prince in that manner that most oblig'd him.

OROONOKO

As we were coming up again, we met with some *Indians* of strange Aspects; that is, of a larger size, and other sort of Features, than those of our Country. Our *Indian Slaves*, that row'd us, ask'd 'em some Questions; but they could not understand us, but shew'd us a long cotton String, with several Knots on it, and told us, they had been coming from the Mountains so many Moons as there were Knots: they were habited in Skins of a strange Beast, and brought along with 'em Bags of Gold-Dust; which, as well as they could give us to understand, came streaming in little small Channels down the high Mountains, when the Rains fell; and offer'd to be the Convoy to any body, or persons, that would go to the Mountains. We carry'd these Men up to *Parham*, where they were kept till the Lord-Governour came: And because all the Country was made to be going on this Golden Adventure, the Governour, by his Letters, commanded (for they sent some of the Gold to him) that a Guard should be set at the Mouth of the River of *Amazons* (a River so call'd, almost as broad as the River of *Thames*) and prohibited all People from going up that River, it conducting to those Mountains of Gold. But we going off for *England* before the Project was further prosecuted, and the Governour being drown'd in a Hurricane, either the Design dy'd, or the *Dutch* have the advantage of it: And 'tis to be bemoan'd what his Majesty lost by losing that part of *America*.

Though this Digression is a little from my Story, however, since it contains some Proofs of the Curiosity and Daring of this great Man, I was content to omit nothing of his Character.

It was thus for some time we diverted him; but now *Imoinda* began to shew she was with Child, and did nothing but sigh and weep for the Captivity of her Lord, her self, and the Infant yet unborn; and believ'd, if it were so hard to gain the liberty of two, 'twould be more difficult to get that for three. Her Griefs were so many Darts in the great Heart of *Cæsar*, and taking his opportunity, one *Sunday*, when all the *Whites* were

59

overtaken in Drink, as there were abundance of several Trades, and *Slaves* for four Years, that inhabited among the *Negro* Houses; and *Sunday* being their Day of debauch, (otherwise they were a sort of Spies upon *Cæsar*) he went, pretending out of goodness to 'em, to feast among 'em, and sent all his Musick, and order'd a great Treat for the whole gang, about three hundred *Negroes*, and about an hundred and fifty were able to bear Arms, such as they had, which were sufficient to do execution with Spirits accordingly: For the *English* had none but rusty Swords, that no Strength could draw from a Scabbard; except the People of particular Quality, who took care to oil 'em, and keep 'em in good order: The Guns also, unless here and there one, or those newly carry'd from *England*, would do no good or harm; for 'tis the nature of that Country to rust and eat up Iron, or any Metals but Gold and Silver. And they are very unexpert at the Bow, which the *Negroes* and *Indians* are perfect Masters of.

Cæsar, having singled out these Men from the Women and Children, made an Harangue to 'em, of the Miseries and Ignominies of Slavery; counting up all their Toils and Sufferings, under such Loads, Burdens and Drudgeries, as were fitter for Beasts than Men; senseless Brutes, than human Souls. He told 'em, it was not for Days, Months or Years, but for Eternity; there was no end to be of their Misfortunes: They suffer'd not like Men, who might find a Glory and Fortitude in Oppression; but like Dogs, that lov'd the Whip and Bell, and fawn'd the more they were beaten: That they had lost the divine Quality of Men, and were become insensible Asses, fit only to bear: nay, worse; an Ass, or Dog, or Horse, having done his Duty, could lie down in retreat, and rise to work again, and while he did his Duty, indur'd no Stripes; but Men, villanous, senseless Men, such as they, toil'd on all the tedious Week till *Black Friday*: and then, whether they work'd or not, whether they were faulty or meriting, they, promiscuously, the innocent with the guilty, suffer'd the infamous Whip, the sordid Stripes, from their Fellow-Slaves, till their Blood trickled from all Parts of their Body; Blood, whose every Drop ought to be revenged with a Life of some of those Tyrants that impose it. *And why* (said he) *my dear Friends and Fellow-sufferers, should we be Slaves to an unknown People? Have they vanquished us nobly in Fight? Have they won us in Honourable Battle? And are we by the Chance of War become their Slaves? This wou'd not anger a noble Heart; this would not animate a Soldier's Soul: no, but we are bought and sold like Apes or Monkeys, to be the sport of Women, Fools and Cowards; and the Support of Rogues and Runagades, that have abandoned their own Countries for Rapine, Murders, Theft and Villanies. Do you not hear every day how they upbraid each other with Infamy of Life, below the wildest Salvages? And shall we render Obedience to such a degenerate Race, who have no one human Vertue left, to distinguish them from the vilest Creatures? Will you, I say, suffer the Lash from such hands?* They all reply'd with one accord, *No, No, No;* Cæsar *has spoke like a great Captain, like a great King.*

After this he would have proceeded, but was interrupted by a tall *Negroe* of some more Quality than the rest, his Name was *Tuscan*; who bowing at the feet of *Cæsar*, cry'd, *My Lord, we have listen'd with Joy and Attention to what you have said; and, were we only Men, would follow so great a Leader through the World: But Oh! consider we are Husbands, and Parents too, and have things more dear to us than Life; our Wives and Children, unfit for Travel in those unpassable Woods, Mountains and Bogs. We have not only difficult Lands to overcome, but Rivers to wade, and Mountains to encounter; ravenous Beasts of Prey.*——To this *Cæsar* reply'd, *That Honour was the first Principle in Nature, that was to be obey'd; but as no Man would pretend to that, without all the Acts of Vertue, Compassion, Charity, Love, Justice, and Reason; he found it not inconsistent with that, to take equal care of their Wives and Children, as they wou'd of themselves; and that he did not design,*

when he led them to Freedom, and glorious Liberty, that
they shou'd leave that better part of themselves to perish
by the hand of the Tyrant's Whip: But if there were a
Woman among them so degenerate from Love and Vertue,
to chuse Slavery before the pursuit of her Husband, and
with the hazard of her Life, to share with him in his
Fortunes; that such a one ought to be abandoned, and
left as a Prey to the common Enemy.

To which they all agreed—and bowed. After this,
he spoke of the impassable Woods and Rivers; and
convinced them, the more Danger the more Glory. He
told them, that he had heard of one *Hannibal*, a great
Captain, had cut his way through Mountains of solid
Rocks; and should a few Shrubs oppose them, which
they could fire before 'em? No, 'twas a trifling Excuse
to Men resolved to die, or overcome. As for Bogs, they
are with a little Labour filled and harden'd; and the
Rivers could be no Obstacle, since they swam by Nature,
at least by Custom, from the first hour of their Birth:
That when the Children were weary, they must carry
them by turns, and the Woods and their own Industry
wou'd afford them Food. To this they all assented
with Joy.

Tuscan then demanded, what he would do: He said
they would travel towards the Sea, plant a new Colony,
and defend it by their Valour; and when they could
find a Ship, either driven by stress of Weather, or
guided by Providence that way, they wou'd seize it,
and make it a Prize, till it had transported them to
their own Countries: at least they should be made free in
his Kingdom, and be esteem'd as his Fellow-Sufferers,
and Men that had the Courage and the Bravery to
attempt, at least, for Liberty; and if they dy'd in the
Attempt, it would be more brave, than to live in
perpetual Slavery.

They bow'd and kiss'd his Feet at this Resolution,
and with one accord vow'd to follow him to death;
and that Night was appointed to begin their march.
They made it known to their Wives, and directed them

to tie their Hamaca about their Shoulders, and under
their Arm, like a Scarf, and to lead their Children that
could go, and carry those that could not. The Wives,
who pay an entire Obedience to their Husbands, obey'd,
and stay'd for 'em where they were appointed: The
Men stay'd but to furnish themselves with what
defensive Arms they could get; and all met at the
Rendezvouz, where *Cæsar* made a new encouraging
Speech to 'em, and led 'em out.

But as they cou'd not march far that night, on
Monday early, when the Overseers went to call 'em
all together, to go to work, they were extremely surprized, to find not one upon the Place, but all fled with
what Baggage they had. You may imagine this News
was not only suddenly spread all over the Plantation,
but soon reached the neighbouring ones; and we had
by Noon about 600 Men, they call the Militia of the
Country, that came to assist us in the pursuit of the
Fugitives: but never did one see so comical an Army
march forth to War. The Men of any Fashion would
not concern themselves, tho it were almost the Common
Cause; for such Revoltings are very ill Examples, and
have very fatal Consequences oftentimes, in many
Colonies: But they had a Respect for *Cæsar*, and all
hands were against the *Parhamites* (as they called those
of *Parham-Plantation*) because they did not in the first
place love the Lord-Governour; and secondly, they
would have it, that *Cæsar* was ill used, and baffled with:
and 'tis not impossible but some of the best in the
Country was of his Council in this Flight, and depriving
us of all the Slaves; so that they of the better sort wou'd
not meddle in the matter. The Deputy-Governour, of
whom I have had no great occasion to speak, and who
was the most fawning fair-tongu'd Fellow in the World,
and one that pretended the most Friendship to *Cæsar*,
was now the only violent Man against him; and though
he had nothing, and so need fear nothing, yet talked and
looked bigger than any Man. He was a Fellow, whose
Character is not fit to be mentioned with the worst of

the Slaves: This Fellow would lead his Army forth to
meet *Cæsar*, or rather to pursue him. Most of their
Arms were of those sort of cruel Whips they call *Cat
with nine Tails*; some had rusty useless Guns for shew;
others old Basket Hilts, whose Blades had never seen
the Light in this Age; and others had long Staffs and
Clubs. Mr. *Trefry* went along, rather to be a Mediator
than a Conqueror in such a Battle; for he foresaw and
knew, if by fighting they put the Negroes into despair,
they were a sort of sullen Fellows, that would drown or
kill themselves before they would yield; and he advis'd
that fair means was best: But *Byam* was one that
abounded in his own Wit, and would take his own
Measures.

It was not hard to find these Fugitives; for as they
fled, they were forced to fire and cut the Woods before
'em: so that night or day they pursu'd 'em by the
Light they made, and by the Path they had cleared.
But as soon as *Cæsar* found he was pursu'd, he put
himself in a posture of Defence, placing all the Women
and Children in the Rear; and himself, with *Tuscan* by
his side, or next to him, all promising to die or conquer.
Encouraged thus, they never stood to parley, but fell
on pell-mell upon the *English*, and killed some, and
wounded a great many; they having recourse to their
Whips, as the best of their Weapons. And as they
observed no order, they perplexed the Enemy so sorely,
with lashing 'em in the Eyes; and the Women and
Children seeing their Husbands so treated, being of
fearful cowardly Dispositions, and hearing the *English*
cry out, *Yield, and Live! Yield, and be Pardoned!*
they all run in amongst their Husbands and Fathers,
and hung about them, crying out, *Yield! Yield! and
leave* Cæsar *to their Revenge*: that by degrees the Slaves
abandon'd *Cæsar*, and left him only *Tuscan* and his
Heroick *Imoinda*, who grown big as she was, did nevertheless press near her Lord, having a Bow and a Quiver
full of poisoned Arrows, which she managed with such
dexterity, that she wounded several, and shot the

Governour into the Shoulder; of which Wound he had
like to have died, but that an *Indian* Woman, his
Mistress, sucked the Wound, and cleans'd it from the
Venom: But however, he stir'd not from the Place
till he had parly'd with *Cæsar*, who he found was
resolved to die fighting, and would not be taken; no
more would *Tuscan* or *Imoinda*. But he, more thirsting
after Revenge of another sort, than that of depriving
him of Life, now made use of all his Art of talking and
dissembling, and besought *Cæsar* to yield himself upon
Terms which he himself should propose, and should be
sacredly assented to, and kept by him. He told him,
It was not that he any longer fear'd him, or could
believe the Force of two Men, and a young Heroine,
could overthrow all them, and with all the Slaves now
on their side also; but it was the vast Esteem he had
for his Person, the Desire he had to serve so gallant a
Man, and to hinder himself from the Reproach hereafter, of having been the occasion of the Death of a
Prince, whose Valour and Magnanimity deserved the
Empire of the World. He protested to him, he looked
upon this Action as gallant and brave, however tending
to the Prejudice of his Lord and Master, who would
by it have lost so considerable a number of Slaves;
that this Flight of his, shou'd be looked on as a Heat
of Youth, and a Rashness of a too forward Courage,
and an unconsider'd Impatience of Liberty, and no
more; and that he labour'd in vain to accomplish that
which they would effectually perform as soon as any
Ship arrived that would touch on his Coast: *So that if
you will be pleased* (continued he) *to surrender your self,
all imaginable Respect shall be paid you ; and your self,
your Wife and Child, if it be born here, shall depart free
out of our Land.* But *Cæsar* would hear of no Composi-
tion; though *Byam* urged, if he pursued and went on
in his Design, he would inevitably perish, either by
great Snakes, wild Beasts, or Hunger; and he ought to
have regard to his Wife, whose Condition requir'd Ease,
and not the Fatigues of tedious Travel, where she could

not be secured from being devoured. But *Cæsar* told him, there was no Faith in the White Men, or the Gods they ador'd; who instructed them in Principles so false, that honest Men could not live amongst them; though no People profess'd so much, none performed so little: That he knew what he had to do when he dealt with Men of Honour; but with them a Man ought to be eternally on his guard, and never to eat and drink with Christians, without his Weapon of Defence in his hand; and, for his own Security, never to credit one Word they spoke. As for the Rashness and Inconsiderateness of his Action, he would confess the Governour is in the right; and that he was ashamed of what he had done, in endeavouring to make those free, who were by Nature Slaves, poor wretched Rogues, fit to be used as Christians, Tools; Dogs, treacherous and cowardly, fit for such Masters; and they wanted only but to be whipped into the knowledg of the Christian Gods, to be the vilest of all creeping things; to learn to worship such Deities as had not power to make them just, brave, or honest: In fine, after a thousand things of this nature, not fit here to be recited, he told *Byam*, He had rather die, than live upon the same Earth with such Dogs. But *Trefry* and *Byam* pleaded and protested together so much, that *Trefry* believing the Governour to mean what he said, and speaking very cordially himself, generously put himself into *Cæsar's* hands, and took him aside, and persuaded him, even with Tears, to live, by surrendering himself, and to name his Conditions. *Cæsar* was overcome by his Wit and Reasons, and in consideration of *Imoinda*: and demanding what he desired, and that it should be ratify'd by their Hands in Writing, because he had perceived that was the common way of Contract between Man and Man amongst the Whites; all this was performed, and *Tuscan's* Pardon was put in, and they surrender'd to the Governour, who walked peaceably down into the Plantation with them, after giving order to bury their Dead. *Cæsar* was very much toil'd with the Bustle of

OROONOKO

the Day, for he had fought like a Fury; and what Mischief was done, he and *Tuscan* performed alone; and gave their Enemies a fatal Proof, that they durst do any thing, and fear'd no mortal Force.

But they were no sooner arrived at the Place where all the Slaves receive their Punishments of Whipping, but they laid hands on *Cæsar* and *Tuscan*, faint with Heat and Toil; and surprizing them, bound them to two several Stakes, and whipped them in a most deplorable and inhuman manner, rending the very Flesh from their Bones, especially *Cæsar*, who was not perceived to make any Moan, or to alter his Face, only to roll his Eyes on the faithless Governour, and those he believed guilty, with Fierceness and Indignation; and to compleat his Rage, he saw every one of those Slaves, who but a few days before ador'd him as something more than mortal, now had a Whip to give him some Lashes, while he strove not to break his Fetters; though if he had, it were impossible: but he pronounced a Woe and Revenge from his Eyes, that darted Fire, which was at once both awful and terrible to behold.

When they thought they were sufficiently revenged on him, they unty'd him, almost fainting with loss of Blood, from a thousand Wounds all over his Body; from which they had rent his Clothes, and led him bleeding and naked as he was, and loaded him all over with Irons, and then rubb'd his Wounds, to compleat their Cruelty, with *Indian* Pepper, which had like to have made him raving mad; and, in this Condition made him so fast to the Ground, that he could not stir, if his Pains and Wounds would have given him leave. They spared *Imoinda*, and did not let her see this Barbarity committed towards her Lord, but carry'd her down to *Parham*, and shut her up; which was not in kindness to her, but for fear she should die with the sight, or miscarry, and then they should lose a young Slave, and perhaps the Mother.

You must know, that when the News was brought on *Monday* Morning, that *Cæsar* had betaken himself to the Woods, and carry'd with him all the Negroes, we were possess'd with extreme Fear, which no Persuasions could dissipate, that he would secure himself till night, and then, that he would come down and cut all our Throats. This Apprehension made all the Females of us fly down the River, to be secured; and while we were away, they acted this Cruelty; for I suppose I had Authority and Interest enough there, had I suspected any such thing, to have prevented it: but we had not gone many Leagues, but the News overtook us, that *Cæsar* was taken and whipped like a common Slave. We met on the River with Colonel *Martin*, a Man of great Gallantry, Wit, and Goodness, and whom I have celebrated in a Character of my new Comedy, by his own Name, in memory of so brave a Man: He was wise and eloquent, and, from the Fineness of his Parts, bore a great sway over the Hearts of all the Colony: He was a Friend to *Cæsar*, and resented this false dealing with him very much. We carry'd him back to *Parham*, thinking to have made an Accommodation; when he came, the first News we heard, was, That the Governour was dead of a Wound *Imoinda* had given him; but it was not so well. But it seems, he would have the Pleasure of beholding the Revenge he took on *Cæsar*; and before the cruel Ceremony was finished, he dropt down; and then they perceived the Wound he had on his Shoulder was by a venom'd Arrow, which, as I said, his *Indian* Mistress healed, by sucking the Wound.

We were no sooner arrived, but we went up to the Plantation to see *Cæsar*; whom we found in a very miserable and unexpressible Condition; and I have a thousand times admired how he lived in so much tormenting Pain. We said all things to him, that Trouble, Pity and Good-Nature could suggest, protesting our Innocency of the Fact, and our Abhorrence of such Cruelties; making a thousand Professions and Services to him, and begging as many Pardons for the Offenders, till we said so much, that he believed we had no hand in his ill Treatment: but told us, He could never pardon

Byam; as for *Trefry*, he confess'd he saw his Grief and
Sorrow for his Suffering, which he could not hinder, but
was like to have been beaten down by the very Slaves,
for speaking in his defence: But for *Byam*, who was
their Leader, their Head—and shou'd, by his Justice
and Honour, have been an Example to 'em—for him he
wished to live to take a dire revenge of him; and said,
*It had been well for him, if he had sacrificed me instead
of giving me the contemptible Whip.* He refused to talk
much; but begging us to give him our Hands, he took
them, and protested never to lift up his, to do us any
harm. He had a great Respect for Colonel *Martin*, and
always took his Counsel like that of a Parent; and
assured him, he would obey him in any thing, but his
Revenge on *Byam*: *Therefore* (said he) *for his own Safety,
let him speedily dispatch me ; for if I could dispatch my
self, I would not, till that Justice were done to my injured
Person, and the Contempt of a Soldier : No, I would not
kill my self, even after a Whipping, but will be content to
live with that Infamy, and be pointed at by every grinning
Slave, till I have compleated my Revenge ; and then you
shall see, that* Oroonoko *scorns to live with the Indignity
that was put on* Cæsar. All we could do, could get no
more Words from him; and we took care to have him
put immediately into a healing Bath, to rid him of his
Pepper, and order'd a Chirurgeon to anoint him with
healing Balm, which he suffer'd, and in some time he
began to be able to walk and eat. We failed not to
visit him every day, and to that end had him brought
to an Apartment at *Parham*.

The Governour had no sooner recover'd, and had
heard of the Menaces of *Cæsar*, but he called his Council,
who (not to disgrace them, or burlesque the Government
there) consisted of such notorious Villains as *Newgate*
never transported; and, possibly, originally were such
who understood neither the Laws of God or Man, and
had no sort of Principles to make them worthy the
Name of Men; but at the very Council-Table wou'd
contradict and fight with one another, and swear so

bloodily, that 'twas terrible to hear and see 'em. (Some of 'em were afterwards hanged when the *Dutch* took possession of the Place, others sent off in Chains.) But calling these special Rulers of the Nation together, and requiring their Counsel in this weighty Affair, they all concluded, that (damn 'em) it might be their own Cases; and that *Cæsar* ought to be made an Example to all the Negroes, to fright 'em from daring to threaten their Betters, their Lords and Masters: and at this rate no Man was safe from his own Slaves; and concluded, *nemine contradicente*, That *Cæsar* should be hanged.

Trefry then thought it time to use his Authority, and told *Byam*, his Command did not extend to his Lord's Plantation; and that *Parham* was as much exempt from the Law as *White-Hall*; and that they ought no more to touch the Servants of the Lord —— (who there represented the King's Person) than they could those about the King himself; and that *Parham* was a Sanctuary; and tho his Lord were absent in Person, his Power was still in being there, which he had entrusted with him, as far as the Dominions of his particular Plantations reached, and all that belonged to it: the rest of the Country, as *Byam* was Lieutenant to his Lord, he might exercise his Tyranny upon. *Trefry* had others as powerful, or more, that interested themselves in *Cæsar's* Life, and absolutely said, he should be defended. So turning the Governour, and his wise Council, out of doors, (for they sat at *Parham-House*) we set a Guard upon our Lodging-Place, and would admit none but those we called Friends to us and *Cæsar*.

The Governour having remain'd wounded at *Parham*, till his Recovery was compleated, *Cæsar* did not know but he was still there, and indeed, for the most part, his time was spent there: for he was one that loved to live at other People's Expence, and if he were a day absent, he was ten present there; and us'd to play, and walk, and hunt and fish with *Cæsar*: So that *Cæsar* did not at all doubt, if he once recover'd Strength, but he should find an opportunity of being revenged on

him; though, after such a Revenge, he could not hope
to live: for if he escaped the Fury of the *English* Mobile,
who perhaps would have been glad of the occasion to
have killed him, he was resolved not to survive his
whipping; yet he had some tender Hours, a repenting
Softness, which he called his Fits of Cowardice, wherein
he struggled with Love for the Victory of his Heart,
which took part with his charming *Imoinda* there: but,
for the most part, his time was past in melancholy
Thoughts, and black Designs. He consider'd, if he
should do this Deed, and die either in the Attempt,
or after it, he left his lovely *Imoinda* a Prey, or at best
a Slave to the enraged Multitude; his great Heart could
not endure that Thought: *Perhaps* (said he) *she may be
first ravished by every Brute ; expos'd first to their nasty
Lusts, and then a shameful Death :* No, he could not live
a moment under that Apprehension, too insupportable
to be borne. These were his Thoughts, and his silent
Arguments with his Heart, as he told us afterwards:
so that now resolving not only to kill *Byam*, but all
those he thought had enraged him; pleasing his great
Heart with the fancy'd Slaughter he should make over
the whole face of the Plantation; he first resolved on a
Deed, that (however horrid it first appear'd to us all)
when we had heard his Reasons, we thought it brave
and just. Being able to walk, and, as he believed, fit
for the execution of his great Design, he begg'd *Trefry*
to trust him into the Air, believing a Walk would do him
good; which was granted him: and taking *Imoinda* with
him as he used to do in his more happy and calmer days,
he led her up into a Wood, where (after with a thousand
Sighs, and long gazing silently on her Face, while Tears
gush'd, in spight of him, from his Eyes) he told her
his Design, first of killing her, and then his Enemies,
and next himself, and the Impossibility of escaping,
and therefore he told her the Necessity of dying. He
found the heroick Wife faster pleading for Death, than
he was to propose it, when she found his fix'd Resolution; and, on her Knees, besought him not to leave her

71

a Prey to his Enemies. He (grieved to death) yet pleased at her noble Resolution, took her up, and embracing of her with all the Passion and Languishment of a dying Lover, drew his Knife to kill this Treasure of his Soul, this Pleasure of his Eyes; while Tears trickled down his Cheeks, hers were smiling with Joy she should die by so noble a Hand, and be sent into her own Country (for that's their Notion of the next World) by him she so tenderly loved, and so truly ador'd in this: For Wives have a respect for their Husbands equal to what any other People pay a Deity; and when a Man finds any occasion to quit his Wife, if he love her, she dies by his hand; if not, he sells her, or suffers some other to kill her. It being thus, you may believe the Deed was soon resolved on; and 'tis not to be doubted, but the parting, the eternal leave-taking of two such Lovers, so greatly born, so sensible, so beautiful, so young, and so fond, must be very moving, as the Relation of it was to me afterwards.

All that Love could say in such cases, being ended, and all the intermitting Irresolutions being adjusted, the lovely, young and ador'd Victim lays her self down before the Sacrificer; while he, with a hand resolved, and a heart-breaking within, gave the fatal Stroke, first cutting her Throat, and then severing her yet smiling Face from that delicate Body, pregnant as it was with the Fruits of tenderest Love. As soon as he had done, he laid the Body decently on Leaves and Flowers, of which he made a Bed, and conceal'd it under the same Cover-lid of Nature; only her Face he left yet bare to look on: But when he found she was dead, and past all retrieve, never more to bless him with her Eyes, and soft Language, his Grief swell'd up to rage; he tore, he raved, he roar'd like some Monster of the Wood, calling on the lov'd Name of *Imoinda*. A thousand times he turned the fatal Knife that did the Deed toward his own Heart, with a Resolution to go immediately after her; but dire Revenge, which was now a thousand times more fierce in his Soul than before, prevents him: and he would cry out, *No, since I have sacrific'd* Imoinda *to my Revenge, shall I lose that Glory which I have purchased so dear, as at the Price of the fairest, dearest, softest Creature that ever Nature made ? No, no !* Then at her Name Grief would get the ascendant of Rage, and he would lie down by her side, and water her Face with Showers of Tears, which never were wont to fall from those Eyes; and however bent he was on his intended Slaughter, he had not power to stir from the Sight of this dear Object, now more beloved, and more ador'd than ever.

He remained in this deplorable Condition for two days, and never rose from the Ground where he had made her sad Sacrifice; at last rousing from her Side, and accusing himself with living too long, now *Imoinda* was dead, and that the Deaths of those barbarous Enemies were deferred too long, he resolv'd now to finish the great Work: but offering to rise, he found his Strength so decay'd, that he reeled to and fro, like Boughs assailed by contrary Winds; so that he was forced to lie down again, and try to summon all his Courage to his Aid. He found his Brains turned round, and his Eyes were dizzy, and Objects appear'd not the same to him they were wont to do; his Breath was short, and all his Limbs surpriz'd with a Faintness he had never felt before. He had not eat in two days, which was one occasion of his Feebleness, but excess of Grief was the greatest, yet still he hoped he shou'd recover Vigour to act his Design, and lay expecting it yet six days longer; still mourning over the dead Idol of his Heart, and striving every day to rise, but could not.

In all this time you may believe we were in no little Affliction for *Cæsar* and his Wife: some were of opinion he was escaped, never to return; others thought some Accident had hapned to him: but however, we fail'd not to send out a hundred People several ways, to search for him. A Party of about forty went that way he took, among whom was *Tuscan*, who was perfectly reconciled to *Byam*: They had not gone very far into the Wood, but they smelt an unusual Smell, as of a dead Body; for Stinks must be very noisom, that can be distinguished among such a quantity of natural Sweets, as every Inch of that Land produces: so that they concluded they should find him dead, or some body that was so; they pass'd on towards it, as loathsome as it was, and made such rustling among the Leaves that lie thick on the ground, by continual falling, that *Cæsar* heard he was approach'd: and though he had, during the space of these eight days, endeavoured to rise, but found he wanted Strength, yet looking up, and seeing his Pursuers, he rose, and reel'd to a neighbouring Tree, against which he fix'd his Back; and being within a dozen Yards of those that advanc'd and saw him, he call'd out to them, and bid them approach no nearer, if they would be safe. So that they stood still, and hardly believing their Eyes, that would persuade them that it was *Cæsar* that spoke to 'em, so much was he alter'd; they ask'd him, what he had done with his Wife, for they smelt a Stink that almost struck them dead? He pointing to the dead Body, sighing, cry'd, *Behold her there.* They put off the Flowers that cover'd her, with their Sticks, and found she was kill'd, and cry'd out, *Oh, Monster! that hast murder'd thy Wife.* Then asking him, why he did so cruel a Deed? He replied, He had no leisure to answer impertinent Questions: *You may go back* (continued he) *and tell the faithless Governour, he may thank Fortune that I am breathing my last; and that my Arm is too feeble to obey my Heart, in what it had design'd him :* But his Tongue faultering, and trembling, he could scarce end what he was saying. The *English* taking advantage by his Weakness, cry'd, *Let us take him alive by all means.* He heard 'em; and, as if he had reviv'd from a fainting, or a dream, he cry'd out, *No, Gentlemen, you are deceiv'd ; you will find no more* Cæsars *to be whipt ; no more find a Faith in me : Feeble as you think me, I have Strength yet left to secure me from a second Indignity.* They

74

swore all anew; and he only shook his Head, and beheld them with Scorn. Then they cry'd out, *Who will venture on this single Man? Will no body?* They stood all silent while *Cæsar* replied, *Fatal will be the Attempt to the first Adventurer, let him assure himself,* (and, at that word, held up his Knife in a menacing posture:) *Look ye, ye Faithless Crew,* said he, *'tis not Life I seek, nor am I afraid of dying,* (and at that word, cut a piece of Flesh from his own Throat, and threw it at 'em,) *yet still I would live if I could, till I had perfected my Revenge : But, oh ! it cannot be ; I feel Life gliding from my Eyes and Heart ; and if I make not haste, I shall fall a Victim to the shameful Whip.* At that, he rip'd up his own Belly, and took his Bowels and pull'd 'em out, with what strength he could; while some, on their Knees imploring, besought him to hold his Hand. But when they saw him tottering, they cry'd out, *Will none venture on him?* A bold *Englishman* cry'd, *Yes, if he were the Devil,* (taking Courage when he saw him almost dead) and swearing a horrid Oath for his farewel to the World, he rush'd on him. *Cæsar* with his arm'd Hand, met him so fairly, as stuck him to the heart, and he fell dead at his feet. *Tuscan* seeing that, cry'd out. *I love thee, O* Cæsar! *and therefore will not let thee die, if possible*; and running to him, took him in his Arms: but, at the same time, warding a Blow that *Cæsar* made at his Bosom, he receiv'd it quite through his Arm; and *Cæsar* having not the strength to pluck the Knife forth, tho he attempted it, *Tuscan* neither pull'd it out himself, nor suffer'd it to be pull'd out, but came down with it sticking in his Arm; and the reason he gave for it, was, because the Air should not get into the Wound. They put their Hands a-cross, and carry'd *Cæsar* between six of 'em, fainting as he was, and they thought dead, or just dying; and they brought him to *Parham*, and laid him on a Couch, and had the Chirurgeon immediately to him, who drest his Wounds, and sow'd up his Belly, and us'd means to bring him to Life, which they effected. We ran all to see him; and, if before we

thought him so beautiful a Sight, he was now so alter'd,
that his Face was like a Death's-Head black'd over,
nothing but Teeth and Eye-holes: For some days we
suffer'd no body to speak to him, but caused Cordials
to be poured down his Throat; which sustained his
Life, and in six or seven days he recover'd his Senses:
For, you must know, that Wounds are almost to a
miracle cur'd in the *Indies*; unless Wounds in the Legs,
which they rarely ever cure.

When he was well enough to speak, we talk'd to him,
and ask'd him some Questions about his Wife, and the
Reasons why he kill'd her; and he then told us what
I have related of that Resolution, and of his parting,
and he besought us we would let him die, and was
extremely afflicted to think it was possible he might
live: he assur'd us, if we did not dispatch him, he would
prove very fatal to a great many. We said all we could
to make him live, and gave him new Assurances; but
he begg'd we would not think so poorly of him, or of
his Love to *Imoinda*, to imagine we could flatter him
to Life again: but the Chirurgeon assur'd him he could
not live, and therefore he need not fear. We were all
(but *Cæsar*) afflicted at this News, and the Sight was
ghastly: His Discourse was sad; and the earthy Smell
about him so strong, that I was persuaded to leave
the place for some time, (being myself but sickly, and
very apt to fall into Fits of dangerous Illness upon any
extraordinary Melancholy.) The Servants, and *Trefry*,
and the Chirurgeons, promis'd all to take what possible
care they could of the Life of *Cæsar*; and I, taking
Boat, went with other Company to Colonel *Martin's*,
about three days Journey down the River. But I was
no sooner gone, than the Governor taking *Trefry*, about
some pretended earnest Business, a Day's Journey up
the River, having communicated his Design to one
Banister, a wild *Irish* Man, and one of the Council, a
Fellow of absolute Barbarity, and fit to execute any
Villany, but rich; he came up to *Parham*, and forcibly
took *Cæsar*, and had him carried to the same Post

where he was whipp'd; and causing him to be ty'd to it, and a great Fire made before him, he told him, he should die like a Dog, as he was. *Cæsar* replied, This was the first piece of Bravery that ever *Banister* did, and he never spoke Sense till he pronounc'd that Word; and, if he would keep it, he would declare, in the other World, that he was the only Man, of all the *Whites*, that ever he heard speak Truth. And turning to the Men that had bound him, he said, *My Friends, am I to die, or to be whipt?* And they cry'd, *Whipt! no, you shall not escape so well.* And then he reply'd, smiling, *A Blessing on thee*; and assur'd them, they need not tie him, for he would stand fix'd like a Rock, and endure Death so as should encourage them to die: *But if you whip me* (said he) *be sure you tie me fast.*

He had learn'd to take Tobacco; and when he was assur'd he should die, he desir'd they would give him a Pipe in his Mouth, ready lighted; which they did: And the Executioner came, and first cut off his Members, and threw them into the Fire; after that, with an ill-favour'd Knife, they cut off his Ears and his Nose, and burn'd them; he still smoak'd on, as if nothing had touch'd him; then they hack'd off one of his Arms, and still he bore up, and held his Pipe; but at the cutting off the other Arm, his Head sunk, and his Pipe dropt and he gave up the Ghost, without a Groan, or a Reproach. My Mother and Sister were by him all the while, but not suffer'd to save him; so rude and wild were the Rabble, and so inhuman were the Justices who stood by to see the Execution, who after paid dearly enough for their Insolence. They cut *Cæsar* in Quarters, and sent them to several of the chief Plantations: One Quarter was sent to Colonel *Martin*; who refus'd it, and swore, he had rather see the Quarters of *Banister*, and the Governour himself, than those of *Cæsar*, on his Plantations; and that he could govern his *Negroes*, without terrifying and grieving them with frightful Spectacles of a mangled King.

MRS. BEHN

Thus died this great Man, worthy of a better Fate, and a more sublime Wit than mine to write his Praise: Yet, I hope, the Reputation of my pen is considerable enough to make his glorious Name to survive to all Ages, with that of the brave, the beautiful, and the constant *Imoinda*.